STYLE

A STYLE STRIKE ROCKSTAR ROMANCE

TONI KENYON

apeople
Publishing

Published by:

Apeople Publishing

Copyright © 2017 by Toni Kenyon

All rights reserved.

ISBN: 978-0-9941488-1-0

Style: A Style Strike Rockstar Romance is a work of fiction. Names, characters, places, and incidents are the products of the author's imagination or are used fictitiously. Any resemblance to actual events, locales, or persons, living or dead, is entirely coincidental.

For Kevin - A great love

INTRODUCTION

Author note: I live in New Zealand and I write in British English. Here in New Zealand we have **footpaths** not sidewalks and **taps** not faucets. We talk about the flavour of ice cream and the colour of the sky. I apologise in advance if you find any of our idiosyncrasies confusing and I hope you enjoy your visit to my homeland. Feel free to email me if there's something you need me to explain—I'll do my best and be happy to oblige.

What happens in Vegas stays in Vegas—unless it follows you home.

All Ashley Jacobs wants to do is forget about the Get Rocked! In Vegas Festival and get on with her life. Unfortunately, the one night she spent in the arms of British band, Style Strike's bad boy bass player, Paul Gray makes that simple wish impossible. She's brought home more than memories. What should have been a fun fling before she settled into her orderly life has gone awry. To her horror, Ashley's entire life is turned upside down when she discovers that she's pregnant. She's literally about to be left holding the baby.

Paul Gray's never forgotten that night in Vegas with the woman who wanted nothing to do with a rock star. Style Strike's US tour has gone from strength to strength and his social media star is on the rise. Paul finds himself surrounded by everything he's worked so hard to achieve. His life is awash with women, fame and fortune—but all he can think about is the sensual woman who walked away from him that night in Vegas.

Knowing the tour's about to hit her hometown, Ashley makes the sensible decision to contact Paul. He needs to be told about the baby, doesn't he?

CHAPTER 1

*P*aul

I can't believe it's been over two months since we played Get Rocked! In Vegas. For that entire time I haven't been able to get the gorgeous Ashley Jacobs out of my head.

"Hey mate," Murf yelled from the other end of the van, "get in here. I've only got one cock and there are two girls begging for you."

We'd played another show. I had little recollection of what freaking town we were parked up in. The entourage of vans sat in the car park of the latest stadium.

The nights were all beginning to blur into each other. Pretty much like the women that were moving through the van.

Each evening another dedicated crowd of fans for Sam and Style Strike.

The girls couldn't have Sam, so the rest of the band were a happy substitute. Most of them were happy with the bass player and the drummer.

Not that I didn't have a little of my own fame going on.

Murf and I might hold down the back line in the band, but we were firmly on the front foot as far as the celebrity stakes were concerned. My social media escapades and Sam's success in the States had rocketed us all into the stratosphere.

I can't decide whether I want to take Murf up on his invitation, or whether or not I'd like to sit the action out tonight.

I thought I saw her in the crowd.

Ashley.

The woman who has haunted my thoughts since the night we spent together in Vegas.

I can't get her out of my mind—no matter how hard I try.

Everywhere I look in the crowd I see her.

I know she won't be there because she doesn't do rock concerts.

But she did do me.

That one night in Vegas.

A night I can't get out of my mind.

An attractive, scantily clad brunette who's a little on the skinny side saunters down the van towards me.

Murf's sent out reinforcements.

She has a bottle of the best champagne in her hand and she's drinking directly from it. She stops in front of me. I can smell the scent of her skin from here, a mixture of sweet coconut oil and something else.

Lust? Desire? Excitement maybe.

She puts her mouth around the neck of the bottle suggestively and looks at me. Big doe eyes full of promise.

Despite my own misgivings and my own thoughts, my treacherous cock twitches.

"Are you coming to join us, or are you going to sit out here all night being a sour puss?" She slides into the seat next to me, presses the champagne bottle to my mouth. I tip it up and drain a large portion of the contents. The bubbles make my nose twitch.

If I can't have the girl that keeps haunting my thoughts, then I can't see any reason why I shouldn't have what's on offer in front of me. It's been like this every night on tour—a smorgasbord of attentive and willing women.

I'm a slut. I have no self-control.

"You were great on stage tonight," she purrs as she slips her hand under my shirt. Her nails rake my abs and I feel my cock fill.

I allow the sensations of lust to take control—shutting down my rational thoughts, pushing memories to the back of my mind. I do what I've always done so well, focus on the moment and fuck everything else.

I slip my hand around the globe of her full breast. I can't remember the girl's name, but I feel her nipple harden in my palm.

She tilts her head back, offering me her throat. Opening herself to me.

It's all too easy.

But I've given up trying to fight it.

She takes my hand and leads me to the rear of the van where I find Murf and another girl lying naked on the bed.

"I'm glad you took the time to join us," Murf grinned as he allowed the other girl to roll a condom down his erect cock. "Girls, he's wearing too much."

Suddenly there's a bottle of champagne thrust at me and four hands are on my body.

I'm being peeled out of my shirt.

My jeans are tugged down and I feel the brunette's hand on my rock hard cock.

She makes good her promise and her lips closely follow.

I close my eyes and pour as much of the champagne

down my throat as I can, lost in the decadence of another night on the road.

————

I feel as if I've been run over by a truck. Instead, I'm inside of a moving one.

Our driver, Lionel must already be at the helm. I have no idea how long we've been on the road, but I know we're on our way to another show.

I look around the devastation of the small room.

There's another name, number and email address scrawled on a scrap of paper at the side of the bed. I pick it up and throw it in the rubbish where sit the remains of a number of used condoms. Bottles litter the room. I don't know how much Murf drank last night, but I'm a cheap drunk. It doesn't take much to push me over the edge and for the night to turn into a blur of colour and sensation.

I pick my phone up off the floor to see if I've taken video of anything that might be of some use to me. It helps me put the night back together again when I see it the next morning in pictures.

I still have fans and I still have an obligation to ensure that they see something that's reasonable.

I also have a no posting while drunk or drugged policy. It's too much to risk being thrown off the tour by Sam's brother, Julian. He may not be with us every night, but he keeps a close eye on what's happening. One wrong move and me and Murf will be consigned back to busking in the Tubes in London.

There's a couple of reasons I'm not going to let that happen.

Trying to look at the screen to see what I've filmed

combined with the motion of the moving truck bring on a wave of nausea.

I shrug on the jeans from last night and make my way out into the main part of the van—stopping on the way to have a piss in the cubicle toilet.

I find Murf and Griff sitting at the table drinking coffee and looking chipper.

"Look at the state of you," Murf chuckled, "you've got no staying power."

"Put some fucking clothes on man, or take a shower," Griff said, staring at my bare chest, "you got lipstick competing with your ink."

"I nearly puked my guts up pissing," I replied. "I'm not standing in there and trying to shower. You can get fucked."

Griff looked as if he could step on stage any moment. Murf, on the other hand, looked as rough as I felt.

"Give me some of that coffee," I demanded.

"I don't know how you slept through the noise he was making last night," Murf said to Griff.

"Fuck up," I didn't want to be reminded about last night, or the night before, or the night before that.

I dug around in the small fridge and found a lone bottle of water rolling from side to side. We'd completely cleared it of alcoholic beverages.

"We got anything to eat?" Seeing the empty fridge reminded me of how much I must have drunk last night. Once I start, I don't want to stop and at the moment, I only start because I don't want to think about Ashley.

"Lionel's going to pull in down the road at some truck stop," Griff said taking another swig of his coffee. "Getting some greasy bacon into you will bring you right."

"He was on form with the ladies last night," Murf said. I took another gulp of cold water and wished he'd shut up. If I said anything I'd just make things worse. I needed to ride out the ribbing and try not to do this again.

But then I'd been making that promise to myself every night for weeks now.

The mind was willing, but the body remained weak.

---

*a*shley

The last couple of months had passed in a blur of excitement.

Finding an apartment to live in with Madi. Moving in. Securing my internship with the finance company. I didn't know where the time had gone.

But I'd known for the last couple of days that something was amiss.

I thought I had the flu. Or that I'd done too much and life had eventually caught up with me.

Then I remembered.

That night in Vegas.

With Paul.

I sat here now in my apartment staring at the cardboard box on the table.

This couldn't be happening.

For the third morning in a row, I'd been nauseous. When I thought back, I realised that I'd missed a period. I didn't even want to think about the consequences of that. About what could be happening to my body. My body behaved like a well-oiled machine. But this month—the wheels may have been sticking—I'd seen no sign of my period.

I swallowed hard.

I couldn't believe I could be so unlucky when I thought I'd been so careful.

One night with a stranger.

I sat staring at the pregnancy test kit. It lay beside my cup of green tea and a bowl of half-eaten fruit and cereal. I had the urge to push the damn test kit off the table. I'd eaten next to nothing this morning and I'd called in sick for the second day running. Work were not going to be happy if I kept this up. If I stayed away for another day, then I would need a doctor's note.

"Well there's no use sitting around here worrying about it," I said to no-one in particular, the sound of my own voice reverberating off the stark walls of our partially furnished apartment.

I picked up the box and headed for the bathroom.

I peed on the stick and then put the plastic strip on the cistern behind me and thought about going to wash my hands. When I picked that stick up again I stared at two blue lines in the tiny little window.

Heart racing, my breath coming in short bursts, I scoured the instructions again. Was it one or two strips that confirmed pregnancy?

There lay the answer in front of me. Two strips of blue.

I pushed the stick back inside the box with the instructions, washed my hands and then walked back out into our tiny lounge and kitchenette in a daze.

What the hell was I going to do now?

Rage boiled inside of me, threatening to explode. This was Madi's fault. If she hadn't talked me into going to that ridiculous rock festival I wouldn't have met Paul and I wouldn't have thrown caution to the wind. I wasn't someone who took risks. And yet I'd been dumb enough to take a risk with him that night and look where it had gotten me.

We used a condom for fuck's sake. How the hell could I be pregnant? How did that damn rubber fail?

I wanted to cry.

I wanted to scream.

Instead, I went to my room and pulled open the top drawer of my cabinet. The drawer where I kept the little things. The memory garden of my life. The small book of photographs that my mom made me of my childhood. My first school report card. A picture of me with mom and dad on my graduation day. The framed certificate I held in that photograph sat on top of the cabinet in front of me now, waiting to be hung in my office. Currently I sat in a cubicle with a bunch of other interns—but I knew it wouldn't be long before I had my own office.

I did not need this.

Pregnant!

Fuck!

In amongst the assorted birthday cards and the scraps of my first twenty-odd years of life was the card that Paul had given me that night in Vegas.

For some reason I hadn't thrown it out. I'd kept it. A memory of the evening. Now I had more than just the card to remember the night--a baby. I couldn't get my head around the notion.

I sat down on my bed and reached for my laptop. With a shaking hand, I opened the top and then opened my email.

I hadn't emailed him in the months since I'd seen him.

He probably had thousands of girls emailing him.

I typed his private address and then stared at the box that prompted me to tell him what this email was about.

What should I type? *Hi, I'm pregnant*, or perhaps, *You're going to be a father*. I had no idea what I was going to put there, so I skipped it. I could revisit it later.

How to start the email proper?

Hello.

Hi.

Dear Paul seemed too formal.

How's it going seemed inadequate in view of the circumstances I found myself in.

With trembling fingers I typed, *How's the tour going?*

I didn't even need to ask that question. I'd tried to stay away, but despite myself, I couldn't stop watching his channel. I knew exactly how the tour was going. But I didn't want him to know that I was stalking him online.

My internship's going well, I typed. I wanted to write, *but now it's all been fucked up because I'm pregnant*, but somehow my fingers wouldn't co-operate. And besides, I didn't think that made a great third line for an email.

A little voice in my head said, *But you're going to have to tell him, eventually*.

I told that little voice to shut the fuck up. It didn't have an opinion when I was letting Paul undress me.

Where are you now? Seemed a sensible question. I continued typing, *I'm back in Seattle and I'm enjoying the moderate temperatures, nothing like the heat of Vegas!*

Now I'm talking about the weather.

Fuck!

It wasn't a lot. But at least I'd made contact.

Hear from you soon. Ashley x.

I spent a full ten minutes deciding whether I should put that single kiss after my name. The fact I was carrying his baby probably qualified me to put a kiss there, but I couldn't be sure.

I went to press send but the stupid programme reminded me that I hadn't given the email a title. I went back and typed, *Hello* and as an afterthought I put a smile beside the word.

With a trembling finger I pressed the send button and then I closed the lid of the laptop.

How the hell was I going to get through the next few days feeling like shit?

My brain wouldn't come to terms with the fact that I needed to start looking up how to deal with morning sickness. Maybe I could turn my head to that thought later this afternoon.

For now, nausea raged through me like a rampant beast and I wanted to pretend that the last half an hour hadn't happened.

I curled up in the foetal position on my bed and closed my eyes.

Maybe if I lay here and didn't think about what was happening in my life—it wouldn't happen.

Denial I think they called that.

If denial kept me safe for the next couple of hours, then it would have to do.

But my head wouldn't stop.

Every time I closed my eyes, all I could see was Paul.

He'd not only infiltrated my body, but he'd infiltrated my mind as well.

I rolled over on my back, pulled my laptop back open and clicked on his channel.

The screen came to life and the room was filled with the sound of his gorgeous English accent.

A tiny voice in the back of my mind said, *Maybe you wanted to get pregnant.*

My stomach rolled at the thought and I rushed to the bathroom to vomit.

Denial didn't seem to be an option.

CHAPTER 2

*A*shley
I might have laid there all afternoon and I certainly hadn't had much to eat.

Madi crashed in through my door. The girl didn't understand the word privacy and knocking before entering had never been on her agenda.

"Oh, here you are," she said almost falling down on my bed. The jolt was enough to remind me that my stomach hadn't settled at all. "What's going on?" She looked at me, concern etched on her face. "Did you not go to work again?"

She made it sound like I had some kind of federal case to answer.

I looked up from the hole in the blankets that I'd been hiding in, "No."

"You look like shit," Madi liked to state the obvious, but in her defence I hadn't been near the shower for days and I think my hair had forgotten what it felt like to have a brush or a comb run through it. "You look like you've been on the bourbon for the last twenty-four hours and I know that you barely drink."

I burst into tears.

Madi's face softened. "Hey, hey," she said putting a tentative hand on my shoulder. "What is it, what's the matter?"

"I'm pregnant," I blurted out the words before I had a chance to think about anything else. Then I broke into a fresh set of sobbing.

Madi sat still. I don't think she even blinked. Between the tears and the snivelling she just sat there. Doing nothing.

"Well, say something," I begged as I wiped my nose on my sheets.

She pulled me into her arms and I began a fresh bout of crying on her shoulder. The clothes she wore reeked of the fast food restaurant she'd been working in while she continued to look for an internship. Her parents could afford to pay her rent, but Madi was stubborn and she wasn't going to go crawling to them for money.

"What do you mean you're fucking pregnant? You don't sleep with anyone."

"Well I did," I couldn't help myself and I added, "at that stupid rock festival."

"Oh, god," I heard the dawning of understanding in Madi's voice.

"Oh, god is right." I hadn't been able to think of anything but Paul since I'd seen those two blue strips on the test kit. "How could I have been so unlucky?"

Madi was all reason and street smarts. "Look. You've just landed your dream job. You can't let this get in your way." She was taking the sensible shoes approach when all I wanted was her sympathy.

"What am I going to do?" I still hadn't really thought things through. The furthest I'd gotten was what the hell would I tell Paul? If he ever replied to my email. I hadn't thought about him ignoring me until right this moment.

A fresh wave of humiliation washed over me, followed up

with a dash of anxiety and nausea just to set my stomach on fire again.

"It's easy, you need to get rid of it," Madi said as if we were talking about putting a pair of shoes in the trash.

"Pardon?"

"You heard me," she said. "You need to ring the clinic and make an appointment. You know, he's a rockstar for fucks sake. He's out on the road, screwing a different girl, or bunch of girls for that matter, every night."

Madi's was the voice of experience. I couldn't count the number of rockstars she'd bedded since the beginning of the summer. I knew Madi was telling me the truth, even if it was a truth that I didn't want to hear.

"I don't know if I can do that." I shook my head.

She looked at me with kindness in her eyes. "Of course you can do it. That thing inside of you is the size of a kidney bean or something. There's nothing there. You just go to the doctors and it's over. It's dealt with and you can carry on with your life."

Madi pulled away from me and held me by the shoulders, looking me straight in the eyes. "You haven't fucking told him, have you?"

"No," I said, probably a little too quickly.

"Are you sure?"

"Of course I'm fucking sure." Now I was angry. Fuck my hormones. I couldn't think straight. How had my life been turned upside down? I had everything planned. Getting pregnant before finding a husband and getting married, wasn't part of the plan.

"But," Madi took a moment to think. She knew me too well. "You've emailed him."

I cast my eyes in the direction of the bedside drawers where the card with his email address lay with the rest of the memories of my life. I could feel the burning heat in my cheeks.

"Oh, for fuck's sake." Madi visibly slumped in front of me. "Why did you email him? You said you'd thrown that card away."

"I lied," I said shrugging my shoulders. I had no idea why I'd kept the card.

"You promised me that you'd thrown that card away." Madi looked hurt and I felt bad for lying to her. I'd never lied to her before.

"I don't know what got into me," I said in a whisper.

"Paul Gray's what's gotten into you." Madi said, "and I think you've got him bad." She shook her head, "I can't believe I didn't see this coming. I thought you weren't into rockstars."

"I'm not," I said.

"You were going to have nothing else to do with him. Why did you email him?" The silence hung heavy between us. I didn't know what to say. Madi sighed. "I guess it doesn't matter why, the fact is that you have."

"I spent the morning throwing up," I said feeling sorry for myself.

"Well, that's not going to get any better," Madi replied eyeing me suspiciously. "You're not going to be able to work. Have you thought this through?"

"I've thought about nothing else," I snapped. "I've lain on the bed all afternoon trying to sleep."

"Apart from that time you emailed Paul Gray!" Madi yelled.

I glared at her.

"I spent half the day trying to pretend this isn't happening!" I yelled back. I lowered my voice and looked at my hand, "The reality is it is happening."

"Well, either way you're going to have to go and see a

14

doctor," Madi said. "They'll need to check you out and I don't know." She threw her hands in the air, "Do what they need to do." She stood up, "You're not seriously thinking about keeping this? I mean, you can't."

"I know," I whined. I was beat, but it was the most insane thought I'd been having all afternoon. I couldn't come to grips with the thought of terminating a pregnancy. I couldn't come to terms with the idea that something might be growing inside of me and I could be responsible for killing it. It wasn't how I operated and I knew I'd never be able to get Madi to see that.

Sensing my uncertainty Madi sat down on the bed again and took my hands in hers. "Look, I'll ring the clinic. We'll get you an appointment and you can go and see somebody."

Madi was taking control. I didn't need or want her to take control, but somebody had to do something. I wasn't sure how I was going to get through the next twenty four hours, never mind the next twenty four weeks.

My life had suddenly been turned upside down and I didn't know how to cope anymore.

---

*P*aul

I half lay half sat on the single seat that ran down the side of the tour bus. Murf sat opposite me, attached to his electronic device, drumming a constant beat out on the table with his hands. He could never be still. The drums gave him an outlet for all of that pent up energy he carried.

Griff stared into space. No doubt still pining for Becky. As I watched him, I began to understand his yearning for something that he couldn't have. I'd thought him an idiot for not taking advantage of the women that were being presented to him night after night, but now, something inside of me began to understand why he might not be able to come to terms with the loss.

I hadn't even had the experience of the relationship that Griff and Becky shared, but still, my one night with Ashley had affected me in a way that I'd not been affected before.

Some days I felt like a pining school boy. My emotions hadn't been disturbed like this for years. I'd managed to insulate myself with women and music and my fans.

Ashley had managed to break through my carefully constructed armour and now a part of me had become vulnerable and I didn't know how to put the shield back up— no matter how hard I tried. I found myself looking for her —everywhere.

I was listening to the mellow sounds of The Eagles, the melodic voice of Glenn Frey singing Take it Easy nudging the edge off my post-hangover-anxiety when Ashley's name flashed across my screen.

I had email.

The distinctive chirp in my headphones told me that this was email that had arrived in my private inbox. The one I gave to special people. It wasn't a mad fan from the video blog who had sent me mail. I had a folder of over a thousand emails that I waded through on days when I felt bad about myself. I tried to answer some—others were just too weird and I deleted them.

Women wanting me to father their children.

Women demanding that I come to their home town and visit.

Women offering themselves to me.

Women who had dedicated a book to me, or written a song for me.

Women who insisted that I'd somehow saved their lives.

Some of the messages were touching but the majority of

them were simply outrageous. I decided a long time ago that women who emailed celebrities were either desperate for some kind of stardom, or maybe unhinged.

I blinked twice and took another look at the screen. The message had flashed away, but in my stupefied state I thought that if I stared hard enough at the flat screen, I'd somehow be able to bring the image of her name back again.

I was still a little hung over. Maybe my eyes had been playing tricks on me and maybe it was my mum emailing. She was about the only person who had my personal email address.

I scrolled down the screen.

Sure enough.

Ashley.

My heart beat fast in my chest. I could feel heat climbing my body. I took a sharp intake of breath and swiped the screen and opened the email.

I couldn't believe that she was emailing me. It had been almost two months and nothing. Not a single word until now.

I read the three lines.

It wasn't a lot—but it was contact. She was still interested in me.

For some strange reason that made me happy. For the first time in what seemed like weeks, a sense of hope and optimism washed over me.

I read the lines over and over again until they were imprinted in my head.

"Who's put that smile on your face?" Griff said from the other side of the van.

"No-one," I said looking up and noticing that the interest from Griff meant that Murf had stopped drumming the table and slipped his earphones down around his neck.

Murf made a lunge for my phone, but I was too quick for him. I slipped it in my pocket.

"Fuck off you two, leave me alone."

"Jesus, must be someone who means something to him," Murf eyeballed Griff, "wouldn't you say, the way he's behaving?"

I knew what was coming. "Just fucking leave me alone, both of you."

They were bored and like a cat when it's been sitting watching a mouse for too long, they were contemplating amusing themselves with me.

They came at me, Murf from across the table and Griff from my side. I had nowhere to go, but I knew if I could wrestle them off for long enough, my screen would lock and they wouldn't be able to get into my phone.

Unfortunately, they knew that as well.

Murf made a grab for my pocket.

"Get your hand away from my balls you gay bastard," I muttered to Murf.

"That's not what you were saying last night when we had those two lovelies with us," he said as I fended him off again with an elbow to the ribs.

He fell away clutching at his side. "Jesus, I think you've busted my rib."

"Serves you right," I said as my breath came in laboured pants. I twisted and turned, trying to keep my precious phone away from the hands of my pesky band mates.

As I struggled, I hit Griff in the face with my forearm.

"Take it easy, mate," he moaned, "I can't go on stage with a black eye."

"Well stop mauling me, man," I replied.

Murf, having recovered from the elbow in the chest made another swipe for my phone. "You can piss off too," I said between short, sharp breaths.

"It must be a woman," Griff said.

"He's not normally like this," Murf moaned.

"It'll be that bird he can't get out of his mind," Griff agreed, "you know, the one from Vegas."

"Well there's been quite a few since then," Murf said.

I managed to pull my knees up to my chest. "Will you guys shut up about my sex life." If I had to smash my phone to keep these bastards off it, I would.

"At least you've got one," Griff said in a wistful tone.

Murf looked at Griff. "Well, it's not for lack of willing women, mate. We keep trying to get you along to the party, but you won't have it."

They were having a conversation while I was pinned beneath the two of them.

"Get off me!" I roared.

The command fell on deaf ears as we continued to struggle.

Somehow I managed to worm my way under the table. I had nowhere else to go. Griff had my legs. One swift pull from him and my nuts would be crushed up against the central pillar that bolted the table to the floor.

"Enough!" I screamed.

"Phone." Murf demanded.

I held out for a few more seconds.

The tension tightened on the edges of my jeans as Griff prepared to pull.

"Okay, okay." I made to take my phone out of my pocket, then I threw it across the van to the seat on the other side.

The two of them left me in hot pursuit of the phone.

I struggled up from under the table in time to see Murf hold the phone aloft in triumph. "Aw, fuck it," he said to Griff, "the screen's locked."

I tried to stifle a smile.

"Fuck off you two," I said as I snatched my phone back

from Griff's hand. I pushed it back in my pocket and made my way to my cabin at the back of the van.

Just another fucking day on the road with a couple of jerks, but I wouldn't give up this life for anything. Some days, there was a part of me that wished I didn't have to put up with Griff and Murf's shit.

---

*P*aul

I decided after the performance in the trailer this morning that I wasn't going there again with my phone or with those guys. I waited until we were somewhere safe—somewhere they couldn't rip the phone out of my hand—to have another look at Ashley's email.

We were backstage, waiting for sound check. Usually, I had no idea where we were. There was a notice pinned to the wall reminding Sam which city we were in. I hadn't taken much notice on tour, one backstage set up was much like another.

But now that I'd received an email from Ashley, I'd suddenly taken an interest in my surroundings.

Ashley lived in Seattle. We were in Portland.

Co-incidentally and as luck would have it, we were making our way closer and closer to Seattle.

I had aspirations of meeting up with the lovely Ashley and replaying that night in Vegas.

If I could find a way to see her with the shit ton of concerts we had coming up, then that's what I wanted to do.

I could already see Murf eyeing up a couple of the girls who were part of the support act's backing group. He sauntered over and sat beside me and elbowed me softly in the ribs. "What you think of those two over there, for tonight?"

"Count me out," I said. I'd had enough of Murf's idea of a

good time after a show. Besides, now I had Ashley to think about again—not that I'd stopped thinking about her for the last ten weeks or so.

"Aw come on, mate," Murf drawled, "we're a team."

"Fuck off, Murf. We're not a team. I'm not into it."

Murf snorted, "You seem pretty fucking into it every night from where I've been lying."

"Yeah, well not tonight."

"It's got something to do with that girl. The blonde from Vegas, hasn't it?" Murf said.

"Shut up about the girl from Vegas," I said.

Murf leaned back and crossed his legs. The two chics he'd been eyeing up walked past.

"Hi guys," they said.

"Well, hello ladies," Murf turned on the charm in an instant.

"We love your accent," the taller of the two said. I was under no illusions that they were on for whatever Murf had planned for the evening. Our accents were babe magnets in the US. All any of us had to do was open our mouth and we were ahead of the game.

Murf stood up and took a girl on each arm. "I think I've got some time before sound check, what say we go and talk about where you girls are from."

He looked over his shoulder, "you joining us?"

I shook my head.

I watched the three of them walking off toward the catering tent. I don't know what Murf was thinking. The two of them looked barely legal. But I guess he was enjoying the attention. God knows, we'd worked hard enough to get here.

I needed something for the channel. With Murf organising his sex life, I sidled up to Griff and pointed in Murf's direction. "Any chance you can keep him occupied with his ladies tonight?"

"Mate, I told you at the outset to count me out of that shit. I don't do group. I've never done group. It's not my thing."

I looked across the backstage space at Sam and Dusty who were ensconced on a couch looking at something together. I envied the intimacy of their relationship. They didn't behave like some of the other jerks I spent my time with on tour. They had something real. That was what I wanted.

Sam looked up and caught me looking at them. He smiled and lifted his chin in acknowledgment. I returned the gesture.

As a couple, Sam and Dusty had their own trailer, but they still spent as much time with us backstage as the rest of the band. We'd all become close on tour. Closer than blood brothers. Dusty was just another one of the guys. These people were my family while we were on the road. As much as they pissed me off sometimes, I couldn't manage these long hours without them.

Sam pecked a kiss on Dusty's cheek. She cupped his cheek with her hand and I sat in awe of the intimacy and love I saw exchanged between them. Then Sam stood up, walked over and pulled up a stool in front of me and Griff.

"How's it going boys?"

"Yeah good, Sam," I replied.

Griff nodded in agreement.

Sam had settled in since we started the tour. The man who sat in front of me now was a veteran. I thought about that first night in Vegas—we'd all come such a long way in the last ten weeks.

I'd worried at the outset that he wasn't going to manage, but things were going well. His brother seemed happy. Julian's approval was all that mattered, really.

I pulled out my phone. "You two up for a little chat for the fans?"

"Yeah, sure," Sam threw his arm around Griff's neck. "I could wrestle this guy into submission." We both laughed as I flicked my phone onto camera and Sam released Griff from his choker hold.

"What's up?" I asked Sam as I trained the camera on him.

"Hangin' backstage with my boys in Portland," Sam said with an authority and confidence that would have been lacking at the start of this tour. There were rumours that the entire tour would be extended because things were going so well. Julian had been in negotiations with the upper echelon of management and we were all waiting to hear whether we'd be on the road for another three months after this tour.

"Looking forward to meeting with the peeps in Portland and making this town rock," Griff added.

"How many pushups on stage for this bloke tonight, do you think?" Sam asked Griff, pointing a finger at me. "Don't forget to vote in the comments," Sam said. He'd become pretty skilled in social media engagement in the last few weeks.

"I think you two should get down and show me how it's done," I said.

"He wouldn't make it to double figures," Sam said poking Griff in the arm.

"Really…" Griff took Sam up on the challenge. "You looking for a thrashing?"

The two of them eye-balled each other, nose to nose. It was making a fabulous video teaser for the show. Sam and Griff made a great scene of carefully preparing themselves to go head-to-head. I counted aloud as they did a version of synchronised press-ups for the camera. By the time I got to fourteen, they were beginning to tire. I cut the shot to me and said, "What do you think? How far will they go? Leave your thoughts in the comments," and I cut the video.

"You're off the hook," I said to them both, "you can give up any time you like."

They both cast a side glance at each other and collapsed on the floor in fits of laughter. I caught the hysterics on camera. I'd cut it in after the shot of me.

"Thanks, guys," I said, "I'll get that up." It gave me an excuse to leave the mob and have some time alone.

After I'd loaded the video, I stared at the three lines of the email that Ashley had sent to me. I desperately wanted to tell her how much I needed to see her again. But, every time I looked at those lines of text, no matter how I read them, I couldn't see anything that matched the degree of longing that I felt.

I knew that I needed to play this cool if there was any chance I could see Ashley again.

I hit reply and began to type:

Hey Ashley,

Great to hear from you. We're in Portland and heading your way.

Then I thought better of it and scrubbed out the last four words, putting a full stop after Portland.

I continued. *Life on the road is tough, but we're having a fantastic tour and Sam's rocking it.*

Off to sound check. Hear from you soon.

PG

I hesitated before I hit send. Was I positive enough about hearing from her? Would she write back to me? Should I put a kiss after my initials?

Fuck!

I pressed the send button before I drove myself insane.

CHAPTER 3

*P*aul

Portland had gone without a hitch. We'd hit the road and arrived early in the afternoon at the next city. The road crew had completed sound check for us, so we had a free afternoon to check out the city. It was something that didn't happen often, so we'd been out as a pack, enjoying the sights and the sounds. Sam had found a tattoo studio and convinced the artists that they should stay open late for us in exchange for free backstage passes.

The show had finished without a hitch and here we found ourselves—hyped and full of post-show adrenaline.

Drinking had been kept to a minimum. The artists said they wouldn't work on any of us if we were pissed.

I'd had two beers and pushed a couple in our guitar technician, Brian's direction. An unusual specimen of roadie. His body had never seen ink and we were looking forward to all being there for his first experience.

He, on the other hand, seemed decidedly nervous about the entire event and had taken those beers from me as if I'd been offering a thirsty man his first drink in a week.

"I'm not getting any kind of poxy Vegas tattoo," said Sam as he peered at the masses of artwork pinned around the walls of the studio.

The boys were all pouring over a set of designs that would suit us all. The tattoo artist, who remained in awe of the entire band being in her studio had earlier suggested that we go with one of her designs that reflected the area.

She'd created some fairly impressive stylised vegetation that we found attractive.

"How about we use this," she said pointing to a willowy blue and green design with hard black edges, "and I put each of your initials in this space in the middle?"

"We need the date as well," Sam said.

"The year, maybe?" she offered.

"Yeah, the year," I said. "We could alway put 'we survived the tour of' in front of the year," I joked.

"Crass jerk," Murf yelled from the other side of the room. He still had a beer in his hand and one of the tattoo artists on his knee. I guessed it would be another late night in the trailer again from the way things were shaping up on that side of the room.

"I vote that one," said Sam.

"It's cool," Dusty added.

Everyone nodded in agreement, more or less bowing to the lead singer's whim. There seemed to be an unspoken acknowledgment that whatever Sam wanted, Sam got. It was his talent, energy and his brother's incredible songwriting that had given us all the opportunity to be here.

So the six of us, Sam, Dusty, me, Murf, Griff and Brian took a seat each with our allocated tattoo artist.

"You in on this?" Sam called to Otis, the head of our close protection team. When we were out and about Otis wasn't far away.

"Nah," the big guy shook his head. He reminded me of an

African American, but he spoke with a perfect British accent. Watching reactions to him since we'd been in America had been fascinating. The moment he opened his mouth, people stopped and stared. It was something I'd gotten used to in London, all races had come together in Britain and the country had become a melting pot of sorts over many years. But to see the expression change on the face of Americans when Otis spoke still tickled me.

Otis smiled the same broad smile I'd seen him use over the last two months to disarm all kinds of potentially difficult situations. "You guys have your fun, I'll sit here and mind the door."

Each of us settled into a comfortable seat and allowed the artists to prepare the canvas of our skin. The artists were young and attractive. I knew at least one of them would be coming back to our trailer tonight and, if it weren't for the way my feelings were around Ashley, I knew that number could well have been more than one.

I watched them set up around us all and realised that they pretty much lived the kind of life that we lived. Working unusual hours, the way they were dressed, with their bright hair, dark makeup, short pants and skirts, leather and denim, they could easily have passed as backup singers in the band.

The young lady named, Jasmine who had donned gloves and begun to work on my body made it entirely clear, with the way she stood close to me and looked at me, that she'd be willing to paw over the rest of my body if I were willing.

Dusty sat next to Sam, the only alteration that the two of them made to the initial arrangements being that Dusty was having Sam's initials tattooed in the middle of her arm and Sam was having Dusty's initials tattooed on his.

I wished it wasn't simply a PG that had been worked into my own design. I thought about the three line email I'd received from Ashley and my struggle to send any kind of decent reply. I wondered how soon I'd hear from her again. I was keen to meet up as soon as we got close enough and I got a break from the tour. I couldn't remember when our next scheduled day off came and I didn't want to make too many enquiries. Alerting Murf or Griff to any part of my plan could spell disaster.

More than anything. I was terrified of putting Ashley off, or scaring her away by being seen as too eager.

I sat back and closed my eyes, waiting for the pin prick of sensation to start running up my arm, as Jasmine set to work.

The cool of the antiseptic wash had lifted from my skin and I could hear the small buzzing—like the sound of a thousand bees—coming from the tattoo guns around the room.

Brian had started moaning already and not in the kind of way I'd been listening to Murf moan for weeks now.

"Shut up you nancy," Sam called from the other side of the room. "You don't hear Dusty whining like that."

"You fricking leave me out of this," Dusty replied, "us girls have a higher threshold of pain than you guys. Child birth and all that."

Brian sounded like he was about to vomit.

"See," Sam yelled, "you're terrifying the virgin over there."

"Don't listen to them," Dusty tried to reassure, Brian. "It'll be over before you know it."

I watched as the artist began to work on Brian's arm. As she touched the gun to his virgin skin, the entire room erupted in a chant.

"Go, Brian! Go, Brian! Go, Brian!"

You never forgot your first inking experience—but I doubted there would be any chance of Brian forgetting his.

The pin pricks began in earnest on my own arm and I closed my eyes, wondering about my own pain threshold as the gun connected with my skin proper. I loved the end result, but I didn't much care for the process and I guessed I wasn't on my own in that respect. I concentrated on the familiar sensations of the needles pushing ink under my skin and lost myself in thoughts of my next meeting with Ashley.

The sound of the buzzing guns lulled me into a somnolent state and my mind drifted toward erotic thoughts of Ashley.

My cock twitched.

I remembered I was in the company of the rest of the band and tried to think about something else.

Anything else.

I thought about the email I would have liked to have composed to her—not the three line idiocy that I sent last. I'd heard nothing further from her since I'd sent that email and the silence worried me.

It had only been a day—but it felt like weeks.

I felt as if I'd been on the road for years—not months.

I composed an email that would tell her that I'd been unable to get her out of my thoughts. How I desperately wanted to see her again. How I sat watching Sam and Dusty and wanted what they had. How I wanted that life with her.

All the time the heat of the ink going into my skin kept cutting into my thoughts.

Brian continued to moan—but I couldn't hear anything from anyone else. I wondered whether I should be worried? Maybe he'd passed out. Then I remembered Otis.

All-seeing all-watching, Otis.

I went back to my daydreaming about Ashley.

I thought about the string of girls whose names I couldn't even remember, who had been through my bed and, for the first time, a dawning feeling of shame possessed me.

I'd never thought of anybody else except myself before. Given no thought whatsoever to anyone else's feelings. I'd just been out for a good time and I'd had plenty of those, but now I wanted something more and that more involved Ashley.

The discomfort in my arm mounted as the artist continued to work. My thoughts continued to drift to Ashley. Before I knew it, the hot sensation on my arm ceased and the artist was covering her handiwork with a clear dressing.

"Keep that on for a couple of days," she said. Then she eyed the rest of my body, "But I guess I don't need to tell a veteran like you how to look after new work."

"Nah," I replied, "it's all good."

"Can I ask you something?" she said as she looked up at me from under an almost white bob of hair.

Here it comes, I thought, wondering how I was going to let her down nicely. I couldn't feign marriage. Julian hated us telling anyone that we had steady girlfriends—not that any of us did.

"Yeah, baby," I crooned, putting my best rockstar persona to the fore.

"Will you feature me on your channel?"

I felt the weight of relief flood through my entire body.

"Sure thing," I pulled my phone from my pocket, sat up and patted the seat next to me. Jasmine ignored the seat and sat herself on my knee.

Cosy.

I did my best. Thoughts of Ashley swirling in my mind as this hot, young thing wriggled in my lap. We talked about my new tattoo and then as we finished. She kissed me.

Brazen.

The only word I could think of.

I'd promised her a spot on the channel. I was a man of my word.

"Hey, Paul," Griff called from the other side of the room, "We're off for a drink to celebrate. Come on." Someone had handed Brian a can of beer and I noticed that the colour had returned to his face in a dramatic way.

"You heard the man," I said direct to the camera. "You coming to join us?"

"Sure," Jasmine said, the hint of a blush framing her cheeks.

"Best little tattoo studio I've visited in the US." I said to camera and shut off the record button.

"Can I really come with you?" Jasmine asked.

"Yeah, sure," I said. Now I felt like a complete prick. But for the first time I needed to be straight with a girl. "But I'm not looking for anyone tonight," I said trying to be gentle. "No disrespect to you, you're a great girl and a fabulous artist."

"No worries," she said. "I had a great time at the gig and I'd just like to hang with you guys some more."

"Okay, no problem." I felt better. I'd put a boundary in place. I could do this.

---

*B*y now, Sam's fame had grown and we were ushered to a private floor in the club. The pulsating tone of the dance music cut through my body. It was always the pulse of the song that I loved. It excited me and gave me energy—that's the way it had always been. Ever since my early days playing in tiny little back street pubs. There was something about the way the sound wound through my body. Almost as if my heart beat matched the pulsing heartbeat of the song.

From where we stood, in the private mezzanine bar, we could see the gyrating bodies of the dancers in the bar below. Circles of blue, red and yellow swam across the writing mass of humanity and they all moved in time to the primitive beat.

I decided it wasn't unlike being on stage standing up here, except I didn't have a job to do tonight. I could relax.

The entire club had been fitted out in chrome and light reflected from all the surfaces—creating an unsettling feeling of hyper-excitement. No doubt the kind of feeling our fans experienced when the explosion of lights announced that the band was about to come on stage. Someone arranged for the bar staff to line shots up across the front of the stainless steel bar. One for every member of the party, except Sam. He stood by and watched the debauchery unfold, Dusty not far from his side. Sam had what looked like a bottle of beer in his hand. Me and the rest of the band knew it wasn't a bottle of beer, but nobody else needed to know that Sam didn't drink.

I positioned myself in front of a shot glass; the lights dancing off the tiny glass containers with the potent contents. Murf lead the charge chanting, "Three, two, one!" On command, the entire line picked up their designated glass, threw back the sharp tasting liquor and then slammed the shot glass back on the bar.

The bartenders filled them a second time and we repeated the process. This time Griff made the call. We each touched our glasses before we threw down the second shot.

The burn of the alcohol radiated from my stomach. It pooled around my middle and then spread out through my limbs, linking with the residual burn in my arm where the fresh ink sat under my skin.

I felt alive and vibrant—full of energy. Adrenaline and pleasure coursed through me. A heady fuel that I'd allowed myself to run on for years.

I closed my eyes, surrendering to the atmosphere, the sound and my base desires.

Jasmine sidled up beside me and pressed her warm, soft breasts into my side.

I opened my eyes and smiled, allowing my lips to slide down onto her willing mouth.

"Let's dance," I said and she followed me onto the dance floor.

Griff followed us both his tattoo artist on his arm. Brian joined us, sporting a silly grin on his face. He kept pointing to the tattoo on his arm—behaving as if he must be the first man ever to endure the needles.

In good humour, the rest of the band followed us to the dance floor, allowing the colour of the light show to swallow us all.

The tattoo artists who had worked on Sam and Dusty danced together—no-one would get between Sam and Dusty as they took the floor. They were a tight unit and I admired that in the two of them.

I danced and allowed the music, the alcohol and Jasmine to take me. I had a sense that I might regret this in the morning—but the morning seemed such a long way away.

CHAPTER 4

Ashley

Nothing made me feel any better.

I spent every morning vomiting and every afternoon trying to get over the shock of waking up in the morning.

I'd been to the clinic, but the doctor said there was nothing that she could give me. I had to tough it out.

The doctor confirmed that I was, in fact, pregnant. My last vague hope that I had some kind of exotic strain of stomach flu dashed by a woman who didn't look much older than me.

The only way to get any relief from this pregnancy was to terminate it and that thought remained as repugnant as it had been from the moment that Madi brought it up.

The kind doctor reminded me that it was early days in the pregnancy and I could still make some decisions about what to do.

The options that she pointed out to me were as unpalatable coming from a professional as they had been coming from Madi.

Having landed my dream job, now I found that I couldn't

actually get into the office on time and if I did manage to get there on time, I spent most of the morning dashing for the ladies room.

I was tired all the time. I'd never been so tired in all of my life. I looked like shit—all pasty and washed out. My brain had turned to mush and I cried at the most inappropriate moments.

My life had become a living nightmare.

I alternately blamed Madi and Paul—not wanting to take any responsibility for the choices I'd made that fateful night in Vegas.

I had somehow managed to drag my sorry ass through another day where nothing had gone right. It was 3.30 in the afternoon when I got the call to go to Mr Jensen's office.

Heart racing. My mind in turmoil. I knocked on the door.

His call to enter sounded like some kind of death knell.

"Do take a seat, Ashley," he said as he lifted his gaze from the papers he was reading on his desk.

Gavin Jensen was one of the leaders in his field. He'd built this business from scratch over the last thirty years and I would have sold my first born child to have a chance to work as part of his team.

The strange thing was, now that I sat across from the grey-haired man—carrying my first to be born child—I knew that there was little chance that I would be able to continue with this internship. The fact that he'd called me here this afternoon, the look of concern on his face, told me more than I wanted to know.

Gavin looked at me with what could only be described as sincere kindness. He shuffled the papers on his desk that he'd been reading and arranged them until the corners were all neatly in line with each other, then he stapled them together.

The sound of the staple gun made me jump.

Gavin Jensen ran his firm the way he kept his paperwork.

Things had to be just so. I knew from the look on Gavin's face that I wasn't cutting it.

He placed the stapled document in a yellow folder and then looked me straight in the face and said, "Ashley, how long have you been with us now?"

"Nearly six weeks," I stammered.

"And, you came with great recommendations, Ashley," he continued, leaning back in his chair as if he needed to put some distance between us, "but things aren't working out as well as I had hoped."

I didn't know what to say. I simply stared, unblinking at Gavin.

He broke the long silence. "We think that you're capable of so much more."

I looked down at my hands. I could feel the damp from my palms seeping into my skirt. My cheeks were flaming. Paradoxically, it was probably the most colour that had been on my face for weeks.

"I've been feeling unwell," I offered in the hopes of explaining my shortcomings.

"Yes," Gavin said, pulling another piece of paper towards him and taking a look at it. "There is the matter of the amount of time you've had away sick. You've used up all of your sick allowance already and some." He put down the piece of paper and looked at me again. "Really, Ashley we're just quite uncertain as to where we go from here. Unless you can commit to being with us one hundred percent and that means from now on, no more days away. Being one hundred percent focussed on the job. All of those things. We're just going to have to suggest that you call short your tenure here."

The sudden realisation hit me. He was asking me to leave —to hand in my resignation.

"I'll do better, I swear." I snapped. I didn't want to let this job go. I'd worked so hard.

Damn, Paul Gray.
Damn, Madi.
And damn that night in Vegas!

He wasn't exactly firing me—but he was clearly writing on the wall.

"I need a commitment from you, Ashley that you're going to be here. I've been looking at your records and in the last," he paused, "well, over the entire time you've been here, if we average out the days that you have been away, you've never worked a full week."

It was damning evidence.

I swallowed hard.

Bile bit at the back of my throat. I wanted to run to the ladies room and vomit.

I dug my fingernails into my legs and concentrated on the sensation—willing myself to stay put in my seat and to calm down.

Gavin carried on, apparently unaware of the severe discomfort that his little speech caused me. "What I'm proposing here is that this week you must make a full week at work. Other than that, I'm going to have to ask you to be on your way."

I nodded. "I understand," I said. "I know I can do better."

Gavin's face brightened and he almost cracked a smile. "Good," he said standing up. "That's what I want to hear. I take it that we won't have to have this discussion again, Ashley?"

"No, Sir," I said as I stood up. It was clear he was dismissing me.

I didn't make it back to my desk. I went straight to the toilet and vomited.

Head down the toilet was not the way I wanted to be conducting myself at work. When I was certain that my

37

stomach had calmed down again, I exited the three cubicle toilet.

The manager of the department, Mrs Henderson stood in front of the mirror, not a hair out of place, checking her lipstick. Her straight pinstriped suit looked like corporate armour. Mrs Henderson gave the impression of being a total corporate powerhouse—which is what I knew her to be. She was the kind of woman that I wanted to be in the business.

I stood beside her. Dark rings under my eyes. At least I didn't have spots of vomit on my blouse, but I looked nothing like the untouchable Mrs Henderson. The woman I aspired to be.

She looked across at me via the reflection in the mirror, with a kindness in her eyes that made me want to burst into tears. "You need to up your game, Ashley if you plan on staying here. I know you've got potential otherwise I wouldn't have recommended that we hire you. Clearly there is something going on in your personal life that needs sorting out."

She applied another layer of lipstick. Checked the edges of her perfect lips and then stowed the tiny capsule in her designer handbag. When she had finished, she turned her attention back to me. "You need to grab this opportunity with both hands because at the moment, you're blowing it."

On that cheery note, Mrs Henderson walked out of the bathroom and left me staring at my own reflection in the mirror. I knew I was blowing it. I'd never felt so out of control in my entire life. This wasn't how I had things planned. I couldn't keep doing this.

I went back to my desk with a newfound determination.

The balance of the afternoon passed in a blur of me trying to comprehend the work that had been sent my way. In every area of my life I felt out of my depth. I had never experienced this sense of thrashing about and getting nowhere before.

Waves of panic washed over me as I headed home on the train.

Just being out in public seemed like an enormous, gigantic insurmountable effort.

People terrified me.

I needed to be at the office first thing in the morning, on time and ready to work and yet I couldn't see how that was ever going to happen with my present circumstances.

When I arrived at our tiny apartment, I sighed with relief and closed the door behind me. I leaned up against the solid door, with its numerous deadbolts and locks and felt safe for the first time all day.

Madi was sat at the breakfast bar. "Jesus, you still look like shit." She had an open beer sitting on the counter top.

"Thanks," I said. I didn't need her to state the obvious.

"Have you decided what you're going to do yet?" She enquired after taking a sip of the beer, washing down whatever disgusting fast food bundle she was having tonight.

"No," I burst into tears.

"Shit. Are we going to have a single day where you don't cry?" Madi asked.

"I don't know," I snivelled. "Gavin Jensen called me into his office today."

"Oh, crap," Madi shuffled on her stool.

"Crap all right," I said echoing Madi's concerned tone. "He said I've got to get myself together or I need to walk away."

"He said that outright?"

"No. But I can read between the lines and besides, Mrs Henderson confirmed it in the ladies room."

"She sounds like a right bitch," Madi said through a mouthful of burger.

"She's not. She's simply a professional."

"Professional bitch," Madi snorted.

I couldn't help smiling. I think it was the first time that I'd smiled all day. Madi may have helped to get me in this mess, but I knew I wouldn't be able to cope at all if I didn't have her to share in my pain.

"Maybe you should just quit," Madi said between mouthfuls, "just until you work out what you're doing."

"No," I shook my head. I'd worked too hard to get this.

"There'll be other jobs, other internships," Madi suggested helpfully.

"But it took me so long to get this one," I moaned.

"So, the next one will be easier. And besides, you can't go on the way you are at the moment. You just can't do it."

Madi was right. I wasn't going to be able to carry on. It was too hard and I felt too unwell.

I couldn't stand being in the same room as Madi with the food smells. Nothing made me feel any better. I crawled into bed—it was the only place I felt safe—the only place where if I remained still I didn't feel sick.

I opened my laptop and watched my email tumbling in. I hadn't had the energy to check it for two days. The usual array of spam. The promises of wealth that I deleted. Junk mail from department stores trying to entice me to buy the next great thing for the new season. Assorted promises of happiness. The only thing that would guarantee me happiness at the moment was being at my desk at 8.30 in the morning.

As I mindlessly clicked through the email newsletters that I had somehow subscribed to, I kept promising myself that I would tidy up my life and unsubscribe. Somehow, that never happened and they reappeared over and over again.

Then I saw it.

His name.

Paul Gray.

My finger paused over the delete key. I pulled my hand back against my chest as if the key could burn my finger. I was terrified that I might hit delete and never know what Paul wanted to say.

I could feel my heart hammering in my chest. My mouth went dry. I didn't expect him to reply to me, especially so soon.

Secretly, I'd harboured the thought that he might reply, but I didn't want to admit that thought even to myself. That would be like admitting we might have a future together.

I banished the idea from my head.

There was no future for the two of us.

He was a musician on the road. Clearly, pregnancy hormones weren't just making me sick, they were destroying my brain.

With shaking hand, I pressed on the email and scanned the contents.

It wasn't a lot, but I could hardly complain. I hadn't exactly written a novel.

I still couldn't decide what I was going to do about the baby I carried inside of me.

Paul's baby.

But he'd replied to my email. He'd made contact. Surely that was something?

I read the words over and over again. They were warm, friendly, to the point.

I put my headphones in my ears and out of almost habit I flicked across to Paul's channel. He'd uploaded another video.

The boys were getting a tattoo. I watched in fascination. Hating myself for doing so. But I wanted to follow his life. I didn't want to admit it to myself, but maybe a part of me wanted to be in that life.

I banished the thought as insane.

Paul's life thrived on insane!

I could see it whenever I wanted along with hundreds of thousands of other women who followed him all over the internet.

What the hell would he want with a girl like me?

I watched, a mixture of strange voyeurism and horror as he kissed a tattoo artist. She looked nothing like me. She was thin, with impossibly large breasts. They had to be implants. No-one had breasts like mine without the rest of the curves that came with them.

Something inside of me reared up—ugly and terrifying.

I hated her. I wanted to cause physical harm to the poor girl.

If I didn't know better, I'd assume I was jealous. I had no right to be jealous. Paul had no idea what was happening with me because I'd carefully hidden it from him.

Maybe now I would have to tell him what was going on.

I shut down his channel and then scanned the news sites and the gossip sites for any new articles on him or the band.

Sam and the band were everywhere. I would never have known where to look if Madi hadn't gone on about them so much before we went to Vegas.

Vegas!

How could one city change my life in so many ways?

Looking at the new articles talking about the fabulous concerts, the women and how well they were being received all over the country just made me feel worse.

I'd watched the statistics for people checking out Paul's channel continue to climb since the first show in Vegas.

He'd become an international celebrity.

I sat here, carrying his child and in danger of losing everything that I'd ever wanted in my life.

The exchange didn't seem fair.

I couldn't stop looking at the pictures of the women who were falling all over the band. I took particular attention over the ones hanging off Paul's arm, with their short, bright skirts, their augmented bodies and their impossibly high heels. Pictures taken at the best restaurants and clubs each of the towns they visited had to offer.

I wasn't anywhere near their league—hell; I wasn't even in the same playing field.

A different girl in every city.

Was I just the girl from Vegas?

I swallowed hard.

My stomach turned over again. I didn't know why I was tormenting myself like this. I wondered whether every girl on his arm had his email address like me.

He seemed so genuine. As if he really cared.

It must have been a good act—or I was simply a gullible idiot.

A pregnant, gullible idiot, I reminded myself.

What had I been thinking? I abandoned the idea of replying to Paul's email and closed my laptop.

I turned out the light. Rolled onto my side and closed my eyes.

Sleep would not come.

My mind raced.

Rolling through the alternative scenarios.

Images of our night in Vegas haunted me.

I must have tossed and turned for most of the night, or maybe I dozed, I couldn't be sure. The alarm screeched into life telling me it was time to get up and get ready for work.

I had to be there at 8.30 this morning.

I put my feet on the floor. The overwhelming sense of nausea was devastating. I only just made it to the bathroom before I threw up.

There was no way I could make it into work.

My life was over.

Well, my chance at working for that particular company was over.

After I stopped vomiting, I made my way back to my room and picked up my laptop.

With no other real options, I lifted the lid and opened Paul's email.

I hit reply.

If you're in my area, I wrote, it would be great to see you. Let me know when you're here. I typed my cellphone number and pressed send before I had a second chance to think about what I was doing.

As soon as I heard the sound of the email leaving my account, I wanted to retrieve it.

What the hell was I thinking?

I rushed to the toilet for the second time this morning.

Madi appeared at the door. "Are you okay?"

"I will be by lunchtime, it usually stops by then." I said as I flushed the toilet and leaned against the wall. I knew the pattern now. There was no way I'd be able to make it to work.

"Can you ring in for me," I said looking up at Madi. Her hair was a mess and she wore a washed out pair of formerly psychedelic pyjamas.

"Yeah," she said looking harder at me. "You sure you can't make it."

I shook my head and watched as Madi went to retrieve her phone from her room. I stared at the peeling linoleum and then lay my cheek against the cool plaster of the wall.

I'd read somewhere that this nausea eased, but it wasn't going to ease fast enough to save my job, I knew that much.

Sure enough, Madi came back with the news that I'd been expecting. "They said that they'll pay you for the rest of the week, but not to bother coming in again."

I felt my chin wobble.

"I'm so sorry, Ash," Madi said and I knew she really was sorry.

I didn't think I'd take it so bad, but despite myself, the tears welled in my eyes and then fell down my face. I started to sob.

"Oh, Ash," Madi said in soothing tones as she began to stroke my hair, "don't cry. It'll be alright. You'll see." She pulled some toilet tissue from the roll and I wiped my snotty nose. "Can I get you anything?"

"I might be able to sip a cup of tea," I said between bursts of blowing my nose. "Have we got any of those ginger biscuits left? I can nibble one of those, they seem to help."

"I'll go and see. Now come on, let's get you back to bed," Madi said as she helped me up off the floor like I was some kind of geriatric aunt she'd inherited.

I felt like an old woman.

How had my life gone so wrong in such a short time?

CHAPTER 5

*P*aul

I woke with another throbbing head and another phone number sitting on the empty pillow beside me. The familiar sway of the van told me that we were well on the road to the next city. The light coming in from the window meant that it must be well past midday.

I was aware of the pain in my head from drinking far too much the night before and the prickling heat of the new tattoo on my arm.

I pried my tongue from the roof of my mouth and groaned. Desperate for something to take the feeling of having swallowed the pillow from my mouth, I looked around, but could see nothing but the empty bottles of booze from last night.

I swore I wasn't going to do this again.

I picked up the shirt I wore last night from the floor and sniffed it. The overwhelming scent of stale perfume and alcohol made my head spin. I dropped it back on the floor and pulled on the nearest pair of jeans I could find.

My life felt like groundhog day.

I stumbled out to the tiny bathroom and relieved my screaming bladder. I was tempted to crawl back to bed, but the raging thirst I had on drove me to find an old water bottle from the rubbish bin. I knew that there wouldn't be any water in the small fridge.

I moved aside empty glasses and pressed the water pump. The bottle began to fill slowly. By the time the bottle was full, I didn't care that the water would be lukewarm. All I cared about was sating the vacuous dehydrated organism that my body had become.

As I slugged back the water, I began to feel almost human again. I checked out the main cabin. It looked as if a large horde of people had been through.

Bottles littered the tiny space and pizza boxes sat stacked on the small table.

I had no recollection of us eating pizza. Jesus, I had to stop doing this to myself. I knew I was having a good time last night. We put on a fantastic show. The tattoos were great and the club. Well, what could I say, I hadn't seen a club like it for months. It rocked. We rocked.

We'd come back to the van with the tattoo artists. One thing lead to another. Even Griff seemed to be getting into the swing of things.

The mourning period had officially passed.

But this morning. Shit. The mornings were killing me.

The only other person out in the main living area of the van was Griff—but only because he'd long ago drawn the short straw and he slept out here. Well, I hoped it was Griff. All I could see was a shape, blankets pulled over where his head must be

He was still asleep. Earplugs kept the noise of the van out for him. He'd sleep through the entire band being in here if need be. He'd been touring for years and has mastered the art of sleeping anywhere.

God only knew what time we all eventually passed out.

I vaguely recall the party splitting three ways. It usually moved to Murf's room, out of respect for Griff and all. But now that Griff was back in action—things had changed.

Murf, nowhere to be seen must still be holed up in his room.

I blamed him for the way I felt. If he didn't insist on bring women back to the van, then I wouldn't be feeling like this.

Although, if he didn't insist on bringing women back to the van, then Griff would still be on his holier than thou mourning period.

Murf had his uses—even if the pounding in my head meant I wanted to beat the living shit out of him this morning.

"Coffee!" Murf groaned as he made his way down the tiny hallway.

"Go tell the driver we need to find a rest stop," I said as I cleared a couple of pizza boxes off one of the bench seats and planted myself not far from Griff's head. Now two of us were upright, at least the driver would stop for us to have something to eat.

Murf made his way down to the front and banged on the driver's glass partition.

It was the same routine every morning. Once two of us were upright, the call was made to find a rest stop so we could get something to eat.

Life on the road. The glamour of eating in truck stops.

As our notoriety grew, it became less and less possible for us to slip inconspicuously into these little truck stops. We had three nights in Seattle coming up. There would be a break from travel and my reptilian brain reminded me, of more importance, a chance for me to try to connect with Ashley.

As my body rehydrated, I thought about Ashley again.

I went back to my bunk and dug around the floor looking for the jacket I wore last night. I found my phone and checked my email.

One email in my private box as opposed to the 867 in my channel inbox that I'd not yet found the time to address.

Ashley.

I swallowed, my mouth dry again, but this time for a different reason.

The contents of the email were short and to the point. But she'd given me her cell number. My spirits lifted. It was going to be a good day.

I was tempted to ring it now, but I knew I'd sound like shit. I threw myself down on the bed. The sheets stunk of sex and another woman.

I didn't want to live like this anymore. I needed to find Ashley and tell her how I really felt. I tore the sheets off the bed and stuffed them into my laundry bag emblazoned with my name, along with the clothes I'd worn last night.

The crew would have fresh sheets on my bed before the end of the next show. My clothes tucked in a clean laundry bag on the end of the bed. All I had to do was get the damn things in the bag and sometimes I couldn't even manage to do that.

The idea of seeing Ashley had given me a fresh burst of energy. I headed back out to Griff and Murf, a renewed sense of hope in the world.

Ashley wanted to see me—nothing would wipe the grin off my face today.

Or so I thought.

*A*shley
Life didn't feel worth living.

The nausea had passed, but the thought that I had lost the very job that I'd worked so hard towards, hurt. That my future had slipped out of my grasp, hurt me even more.

It hurt more than I cared to admit.

Sick of crying into my pillow, I had at least managed to get myself through the shower and eat a small bowl of bland cereal.

Madi had left to go to her job at the local burger bar. It was the kind of place that I was going to end up in. I put my hand on my stomach in acknowledgment of the tiny life that grew inside of me. Why couldn't I just let it go?

Another tear rolled down my face.

I'd spent most of the morning surfing the internet. Trying to work out ways that I could survive as a single parent.

Parent.

I hadn't told my own parents what was going on in my life.

I'd sworn Madi to secrecy and I knew that she wouldn't say anything—it wasn't her way. She continued to press me, in a gentle way. Too much prodding and I burst into tears.

I was reading an article about a woman who managed to maintain a career and be a mother. She talked about how hard it was to maintain both.

My email pinged.

A message from Paul.

I scanned the words:

Hey,

Thanks for your number. I'll call soon. We've three nights in Seattle. We haven't had more than one night anywhere since Vegas.

Vegas! Vegas was where this had all started. I'd started a

job, lost a job and found out I was pregnant since Vegas and he'd spent every night on the road.

What kind of life was that?

I continued reading.

It would be great to catch up since we won't be travelling for a couple of nights. Any chance you can get down to the venue or should I come to you?

PG

He wanted to see me.

For the first time since I'd discovered that I was pregnant, I could feel a small swell of hope growing inside of me.

I made a decision on the fly.

I wrote straight back to him before I had a chance to change my mind.

Hi,

I can make it to the venue. How shall we connect?

A

I was washing my plate out when my phone rang. An unknown number.

"Hello,"

"Hi, how are you?" The deep gravel sound of Paul's voice was unmistakable. The small swell of hope that I had been nurturing in my stomach became a full-blown tsunami of optimism.

He'd called. He really did want to see me. It wasn't just a figment of my imagination.

"I'm great." I lied. My life had never been so far down the toilet, but Paul didn't need to know that—well not yet, anyway. "How's the tour treating you?" I knew the answer, I'd been watching his channel incessantly since Vegas, but he didn't need to know that either.

"It's a tour. Sam's going great. Your people love us." He laughed. The vibration of sound rolled through my body and I felt really alive for the first time since he'd touched me, all those months ago. I didn't want to feel like this. I didn't want to pine for the sound of Paul's voice, a couple of words he threw my way to make my day—but I couldn't change the way I felt.

"What's not to love," I said trying to sound flippant.

"So you're keen to catch up?"

I nodded, "Yes."

"I can arrange a backstage pass for you tomorrow night."

There was a silence. I didn't expect for him to suggest we meet so soon.

"Ashley, you still there?" Did he sound worried, I couldn't be sure. "If tomorrow's not convenient, then any of the next two nights."

"No, tomorrow's good." What else did I have to do with my time? I needed to see Paul and I needed to tell him what was going on. The idea of telling him made me feel queasy. But then, anything seemed to make me queasy these days.

"Great," he said sounding pleased with himself. "I'll make sure that there's a pass for you at the gate."

That part of my brain that I hadn't wanted to listen to wondered how many other girls he arranged backstage passes for. The part of me that kept trying to convince me that somewhere deep inside of him was a decent man, told the rest of my brain to shut up.

"What time should I get there?"

"We'll be there from around two in the afternoon, so any time after that," he said all the world sounding as if he was looking forward to catching up with me.

"Great." I wasn't sure what else to say.

"How've you been?" Paul asked. Did he have half a day to listen to my woes?

"Fine," I squeaked.

Fucked-up. Insecure. Neurotic and emotional.

The acronym rattled through my head.

"How's the job?"

Now I did want to cry. "Oh, they've let me go."

"Aw, that's too bad," he said, "but bonus for me. It means I get to spend more time with you."

Something about that idea, despite how unwell I'd been feeling, pressed all of my pleasure buttons.

There was a commotion in the background, the sound of many voices coming down the line. I could hear someone calling Paul's name.

"Look, I've got to go." What sounded like a note of frustration filtered through his perfect English accent, "but you will come, won't you?"

"Yes. I'll come," I said. I had no idea what I was going to say to him, or how he was going to react, but I'd go and see him.

We at least both deserved that much.

CHAPTER 6

*P*aul

I felt like a high school boy waiting for his first crush to arrive before the school ball. I'm sure I checked my watch a dozen times that afternoon.

The boys had given me nothing but grief since they'd found out that Ashley had been issued a backstage pass.

"Quit your worrying, Prince Charming," Murf said as he swatted my head. "She'll turn up. I mean," he added a note of sarcasm in his voice, "who could resist you."

"Fuck off," I swatted his hand away, but he continued to buzz around, annoying me like some kind of persistent fly.

"You must have checked your watch fifteen times since we got here."

I looked up at the grinning fool. "Don't you have somewhere to be other than here annoying me?"

Murf shrugged and sat down in the chair across the table from me. "That bastard, Griff wants my room. I think I preferred things when he wasn't into bringing chicks back to the van after the show. Can't you talk him into going back into mourning or something."

I shook my head. "Nah. You two fight it out. It shouldn't worry an exhibitionist like yourself. You don't give a fuck who sees you doing the dirty deed."

Murf grinned, his warm smile reminding me why he didn't have any trouble bringing women back to the van. "Yeah, but the chickadee's might care." Murf spun an empty plastic water bottle on the table in front of us. It reminded me of the times I'd played spin the bottle as a teenager back home. The memory amused me and I smiled.

"You don't have to look so fucking smug about things," Murf moaned. "Just because your tenure's secure with your girl coming back stage tonight."

"She's not my girl," I said. I wasn't sure if I was reminding Murf or myself. Things were by no means certain between me and Ashley, but if I had my way, she would be my girl by the end of three nights in this city. I had the seeds of a plan in mind and I intended to make sure that before we left Seattle, Ashley would be my girl.

*S*ound check had gone smoothly—the boys had done another great set up. A late luncheon was being served and I decided to fill my time by shooting something for the channel.

Murf and Griff were having an arm wrestle. With his newfound single man status, Griff wasn't so keen to be spending the rest of the tour sleeping in the living space. He said he needed some privacy. They had decided that the winner of an arm wrestle would have the other private room.

Thankfully, Griff had listened to reason and I'd been given a leave pass for Seattle. Murf had begrudgingly let me out of the room lottery, only after I'd had to admit that Ashley might be someone I'd like to pursue a long-term relationship with—otherwise I'd be down wrestling with the best of them.

"Aw, fuck it," Murf screamed as Griff pressed his knuckles to the table. "Best of three?"

"Fuck off, loser," Griff grinned, flexing his bicep, the bright colours of his new tattoo on the lower part of his arm also coming into focus for the camera.

Murf would be consigned to the living area of the van tonight, much to his disgust and much to the enjoyment of the rest of the band.

"You got a spare room, right?" Murf looked across at Sam and Dusty who were slapping Griff on the back for the benefit of my camera.

"Forget it!" Dusty said, the most charming smile on her face.

"Sam, me old mate," Murf turned his charm on the man who Dusty allowed to believe wore the trousers in their relationship.

"You heard the lady," Sam said, putting his arm protectively around Dusty and giving her a little squeeze. Dusty's grin widened and, for the benefit of the camera, she gave Murf the finger.

"I'm crushed," Murf said playing right into the hands of our fans.

I knew this would make a great little vignette for the channel and, it had the added benefit of keeping me busy while I tried not to think about Ashley.

"Great job, guys," I said after I'd hit the stop button on the camera. "You'll have half the continental US offering you a room after that performance," I said to Murf as I clapped him on the back.

"Yeah, right," he muttered in a good humoured tone before grabbing Griff in a headlock and wrestling him to the ground.

I hadn't long posted the little vignette to the channel before I heard the unmistakable deep tones of Otis' voice as he called me from across the backstage area.

"You've got a visitor," he said as he stood aside and the much smaller frame of Ashley came into view.

I would have known her anywhere. She wore her long blonde hair in a thick plait that hung down one shoulder and she had on a light, knit tank top and a pair of washed out denim jeans that hugged all her ample curves in the right places.

A small faded orange pack hung from her back. I dared to hope that she might have a couple of sets of clothing in that back pack because I wanted her to stay for the entire time we were in Seattle. I knew it was her home town, but surely I could persuade her to stay with me—maybe even convince her to come on the road. There was no shortage of women who'd gladly spend their time with me, but it was Ashley that I wanted. In the split second of seeing her standing there that desire was only confirmed for me.

"Hello," she said as she stepped out from behind the bulk of Otis' body.

"Hello," I sounded like a British mimic. I'd been planning this moment for so long, now I didn't have a clue what to say. I knew I was standing there grinning like a bloody idiot, but I couldn't help myself. "I'm so pleased you've come."

"Why wouldn't I come?" Something that looked like concern crossed her even features. Was that her bottom lip I saw begin to tremble? I rushed forward pulling her into my arms and giving her a huge bear hug.

"I'm not in the habit of asking people to come backstage," I tried to explain, maybe make her feel better.

"Oh, of course," she said, her face brightening.

"I guess I'm not in the habit of coming backstage either." A slip of a smile began to spread on her face.

"You remember the band," I said pointing out, Griff, Murf, Sam and Dusty.

"Yes, hello again," Ashley said greeting the nodding heads.

"Nice to see you again," Dusty said coming over and giving Ashley a huge hug. Ashley seemed taken aback at all the attention.

"Thanks," she said, "it's nice of Paul to ask me back here."

"He's not shut up about you since Vegas," Murf said clearly having it in for me and still sore about losing his room to Griff.

I glared at him. But he didn't take any notice.

"You hungry?" I asked pointing in the direction of the catering table. We had an ample array of food to keep us all fed before we went on stage.

"No," she said, almost too quickly.

"How about a soda?"

Ashley nodded. "Yes, that would be nice. It was a bit of a mission getting here and then getting through the gates out front."

"Yeah, security's an arse, but we need it."

"They searched my bag and everything."

"Let me take that," I said reluctant to release my grip on Ashley, but determined to at least be some kind of gentleman. Show her that I cared. That I could be trusted to look after her.

"Sure." She shrugged the pack off her back and I slung it over one shoulder. It was light. Not a lot in there, I thought. Maybe I was projecting too far ahead, hoping that she'd stay.

"We can take it back to the van," I offered.

"Don't you have sound check or something?" she asked. Didn't she want to go back to the van with me?

"I'm not going to jump you as soon as we're alone," I said, "well, not unless you want me too." My words were rewarded with the spread of a blush across Ashley's too pale face.

"The van would be good," she said.

I took Ashley's hand and we headed for the exit from the back stage area, ignoring the hoots and cat-calls coming from the band.

"Don't take any notice of them," I said squeezing Ashley's hand. "They've been on the road too long. It can make you a bit mad at times."

---

*A*shley
    Paul showed me to the familiar trailer. Nothing much had changed, except that maybe a few more alcoholic beverages had found their way to the tiny fridge.

"I'm sure we had some soda around here, somewhere," he said diving through cupboards and pulling out empty boxes.

"Don't worry," I said, "it's not important." But he didn't seem to be listening.

He'd barely touched me since I'd arrived. We'd stowed my pack in his tiny room and we'd awkwardly danced around each other's bodies in the tiny space. Nothing seemed out of place. In fact, compared to the state of the rest of the trailer you could say that Paul's room was impeccably clean. If I didn't know better, I'd have thought that he'd tidied up before I got here.

All that did was make me wonder what he might have to hide.

Then I thought about the growing life inside of me and guilt pooled in my stomach like a heavy stone. If anyone had anything to hide, it was me.

"Ah, here we are," he said a triumphant note to his voice. "It's warm but at least it's non-alcoholic. If you want a cold one, I could always go and get something from backstage."

"It's okay," I said. Unscrewing the cap and taking a sip of

the lukewarm sugary fluid. At least the sugar would keep my energy levels up. I still wasn't eating much and the thought of the table of food sitting backstage still made my stomach turn over.

I could feel the weight of the pregnancy sitting between the two of us. What I'd liked so much about Paul was his ability to make me feel at ease. He seemed to have lost all of that somewhere in the last two months.

Or maybe it was me.

I'd come here with something to tell him and until I told him about the baby, I was going to feel this intense awkwardness around him.

"So," he said, settling down in the seat next to me, so close that I could smell the scent of his skin. Nothing about Paul repulsed me like being close to other people repulsed me. "Tell me what's been going on in your life since I saw you last."

"Well," I stammered.

"Aw fuck that," he said, tucking his hand under my chin and turning my face toward his so that he could look at me. "I've been waiting to do this for months."

His mouth was on mine before I had a chance to say another word.

My hands, of their own accord, slid up his neck, my fingers taking root in the short crop of his hair at the back of his neck.

He moaned out loud as his soft tongue found its way into my mouth.

A sense of pleasure, one that I hadn't known since the last time I'd sat in this trailer with Paul consumed me. One of his hands cupped my breast, the other trailing across my neck.

Feeling safe for the first time in what seemed an age, I surrendered myself to the overwhelming sensations and allowed Paul free reign of my body.

When our lips eventually parted he whispered, "You're so beautiful," his voice deep and hoarse.

I hadn't felt beautiful for a long time. But somehow, now that I was here, with Paul he changed things for me. He smoothed all the rough edges of my life. Maybe the original connection I'd felt with him in Vegas hadn't been my imagination after all.

This was it. The moment I should tell him. I knew there would never be a right moment. But then I thought about him going on stage tonight. How could he work, with what I had to tell him on his mind?

We sat with our foreheads together.

"What are you thinking?" he suddenly asked.

"You don't want to know," I only half joked.

"I do," he said, stroking the side of my cheek with his thumb.

I leaned back and shook my head, "No. You don't."

"Maybe you can tell me later," he said, "after."

"After what?"

He stood up and pulled me to him again, his lips locking over mine in another mind blowing kiss. His hands found the cheeks of my ass and he pulled me to him.

He was hard. I could feel the length of his cock through his jeans.

"I've never stopped wanting you since that night in Vegas," he said between gasps. "I want you to stay here with me while we're in Seattle."

"Here. In the trailer?" I squeaked.

"Yes," he growled, his mouth covering mine again.

Despite the turmoil in my head, my body continued to respond to the sexual call of him.

I could feel myself getting wet.

I wanted him and I wanted him bad.

Fuck it. I thought. What have I got to lose? I certainly

didn't have to worry about getting pregnant that was already taken care of.

I could stay the night. Tell him tomorrow after the show. Besides, the way my body behaved in the mornings these days, there was little chance that he'd avoid seeing me with my head down the toilet.

Despite the small space we stood in, Paul managed to pick me up and carry me into his tiny, familiar room.

He pushed the door closed and, before I had another chance to think things through, we were naked and I no longer cared.

Paul's beautiful inked, hard body lay against mine and nothing else mattered in the world.

CHAPTER 7

*P*aul

I'd been waiting to get her naked and in my bed again since we'd left Vegas months ago.

Seeing her here now, warm and wet and wanton. It took every single ounce of my willpower not to drive myself inside of her and fuck her until she came, screaming my name.

I took a breath and reminded myself that I wanted to seduce Ashley. Not scare her off. I wanted to take my time—despite my screaming libido's demands. I wanted to explore her luscious curves. Get to know every single inch of her body. Commit it to memory. Make her tremble with need and desire and then satisfy her like she'd never been satisfied before.

All of these things I craved because I'd never wanted a woman the way that I wanted Ashley. I was terrified that if I behaved in the way I'd always behaved that I'd scare her away.

So, I thought about what Ashley needed.

I took my time.

Wallowing in the warmth of her body.

Brushing the pale flesh of her breasts. Watching with increasing fascination as her large, dark nipples peaked. Enjoying the sensation of the tight nub of skin as I suckled each nipple in turn.

Ashley arched her body into mine.

The soft flesh of her belly reaching toward the rough, inked skin of my own.

"You like that," I whispered into her ear before I slipped my tongue into her mouth, muffling any chance she had of answering me.

I took my time. Making her body ready for me. Wallowing in the reflected pleasure each lick, or touch, or stroke generated.

When I slipped a couple of fingers inside of her slick folds, Ashley's back arched off the bed and she shuddered in an almost instantaneous orgasm.

"That's it," I cooed, "come for me, baby."

And she did.

Over and over as I slipped my fingers in and out of her. I kept her on the edge, then tipped her over as I circled her clit. Each circle spiralling her to another orgasm.

"You want me, inside you, now?" I asked.

"Yes," she panted, her beautiful eyes open, pupils so wide I could scarcely see the colour that surrounded them.

I pulled a condom from under the pillow, sheathed my rock hard cock and eased myself inside of her.

Home.

It felt so much like coming home.

I pulled out of her. Took a deep breath and inched my way back inside.

I closed my eyes. Willing my body to slow its compulsion to drive my cock in and out. I wanted to take this slow. Show Ashley how much she meant to me.

Maybe I counted as far as twelve as I stroked my cock in and out with the greatest of care—but the overwhelming urge to take her won out in the end.

I felt her muscles clamp around me as she shuddered to another orgasm.

Despite my desire to make myself last. I couldn't.

I threw my head back and roared as the rush of release tore through my body.

---

*a*shley

    I didn't mean to end up in Paul's bed again.

I had no idea how long we'd dozed together.

I meant to tell him about the baby growing inside of me. Instead, I'd allowed him to play my body. I couldn't even begin to describe the pleasurable sensations being with him invoked in me.

No-one had ever given me as much pleasure as Paul.

I lay in his arms. He'd wrapped his hard, inked body against mine and he hung on as if he wasn't ever going to let me go.

I couldn't decide whether to be relieved or terrified.

How could I let him do this and not tell him I was pregnant?

I reminded myself that it was just a few hours before he was due on stage. I couldn't break this kind of shattering news to him just before he went to work. What the hell are you doing in his bed then? I had to ask myself.

Paul's breathing began to slow. He was falling deeper into sleep.

I think I was falling in love.

I couldn't be in love with him—could I?

A night in Vegas. An afternoon here. Granted, I felt as if I knew him because I'd been stalking him for so long over the internet. But the self-centred, self-serving person that I saw on his channel did not correlate in any way to the warm, thoughtful, giving person who had just spent nearly an hour making my body sing.

Could it be possible to have a simple, loving relationship with someone who did what Paul did for a living?

Was there a chance that we could be a family?

Maybe I didn't have to face being a single parent.

A hammering on the door made me jump and Paul sat upright, immediately awake.

"Hey, lovebirds," a voice called from the other side of the door.

"Fuck off, Murf," Paul yelled back.

"We're on in an hour. If you want some grub come get it now."

"We'll be right out," Paul said swinging his long legs off the bed and staring at the floor as if he were reorienting himself with where we were.

He yawned and scrubbed at his eyes with his hands.

Then he turned to me, looking across the muscular curve of his shoulder. His face lit up when he caught my eye. "You hungry?"

"Always for you," I said. It seemed pointless to hide my feelings from him, or myself, anymore.

He brushed his thumb across my lips and then leaned in and kissed them.

"You're fantastic, you know that?"

I shook my head, "Not really."

"You are," he insisted. Then he stood up and started to dress.

"Aren't you going to shower?" I asked.

Paul shook his head, "Nah. I want the scent of you on my body when I'm up on stage."

"Ew!"

"Does that idea appal you?" He crawled back on the bed, leaning over my body and then licked me from my collar bone, up the length of my neck.

A fresh bolt of desire ran through my body and I shivered.

"You'd like me to fuck you again," he said a triumphant tone to his voice, "but you'll have to wait until after the show." He climbed off the bed and pulled on a black t-shirt that hugged his muscles in all the right places.

I couldn't decide whether I was turned on by his attitude, or whether I should be pissed off by his arrogance.

I went to get out of bed.

"Don't move," he ordered.

He came back to bed with his phone.

"You're not filming me and you're not putting me up on that channel." I said pulling the sheet over my head.

"I promise I won't," he said. "But I want something for me."

I peeked out from under the sheet. "How do I know you can be trusted?"

His mouth was on mine in an instant. Hot. Demanding.

"You have to trust me," he replied. "I still don't understand why you won't be on my channel. I want the entire world to know that you're here in my bed."

"Well, I don't."

He shrugged. "Have it your way then, but you still have to let me film us. Just for me." He lay down beside me, nibbling at my ear. Making little mewling noises and whispering please. I couldn't say no.

"I'll hurt you if anything you film ever makes it to your channel," I said.

"Promise?" He asked, his voice full of hope.

"You're a pervert."

"Only for you," he said as he arranged the sheet across my body. I pulled it higher up, almost to my neck.

"Look a little sexy, just for me," he begged.

I sighed and allowed him to pull the sheet far to far down the top of my chest, but still high enough that I had a modicum of dignity.

"Are you filming?"

"I have been the entire time," he said, a massive grin on his face.

"I swear," I said leaning up and over him.

"You look so sexy when you get mad with me," he growled. "Now, for the record," he said pulling me across his hard, inked chest, "tell me what you liked best about the way I made you come this afternoon."

"I'll tell you no such thing," I said. I could feel the heat of my blush racing up my face.

"Anyone ever tell you how gorgeous you look when you're embarrassed?" He asked.

"No," I said, "and I think you need to go and have a shower."

"I told you," just before he licked my face, "I want to smell of you when I'm on stage."

"Then you need to shut that thing off and let me get in the shower."

"Off you go," he said, an evil glint in his eye.

"Give me that," I grabbed for the phone, trying to press the button that stopped it from recording.

"Ah, ah, ah," he said holding the phone just out of my reach.

"I'm not moving from here," I said pulling the sheet up tighter around me, "until you give me that phone."

"Then you're going to be here all afternoon," he said a note of arrogance in his voice.

"Paul!"

He shivered. "I like it when you say my name like that. But I think I prefer it when you scream my name when you're coming."

There was another hammering on the door. "Get out here!" a voice yelled.

"Fuck off!" Paul yelled back. "Now," he said turning his attention back to me, "where were we?"

"You were giving me that phone," I said in the sweetest tone I could muster.

"I need a kiss and then I'll give it to you," he said leaning in close to me.

Our lips touched.

His tongue found its way into my mouth and I forgot about anything except Paul. My body's response to him terrified and exhilarated me all at the same time.

"Here you go," he said handing me the phone, "a deal's a deal and I always deliver on my promises."

He was so sure of himself. That and his arrogance terrified me.

"Off you go," he said pulling the sheet from my body now that his phone was firmly in my hand, "you need to shower and freshen up before the show?" And there he went again, concern overriding arrogance before I had a chance to change my mind about him.

"There you are," I threw the phone back to him when I was sure that he couldn't turn it on before I got out of the room.

He pulled a towel from a laundry bag and threw it at me. "Shower's on your left. Don't be too long or they'll send another search party looking for us."

"They won't still be out there?" I didn't like the idea of walking around the trailer half naked in front of strangers.

"You've got nothing that they haven't seen plenty of on

the road, baby," Paul replied, "but if it makes you feel better, I'll check that they've gone."

I didn't like the thought of a parade of naked women through the trailer. It took me a moment to realise that was because the idea of Paul with anyone else made me jealous.

I had no right to be jealous. We'd made no commitments to each other.

Other than you're pregnant, a tiny voice reminded me.

I told it to shut up.

Paul came back in the room and said, "The coast's clear. We have the van to ourselves."

I wrapped the towel around my body and made my way down the tiny hallway to the even smaller shower cubicle.

How these men lived like this for weeks on end, I couldn't imagine. On top of each other. People coming and going. Different cities. Different women.

The idea appalled me. I could barely turn around in the shower space, but I quickly freshened myself up. Dried myself as best as I could in the cramped space and made my way back to Paul.

I had no idea what the rest of the evening would entail, but I knew one thing.

I had to tell him about the baby—no matter what.

CHAPTER 8

*P*aul

We were fucking smashing it on stage.

The crowd were going wild. Every concert on the tour had seen an increasing level of excitement. From the outset Sam had something amazing going on and the American crowds had welcomed him with open arms.

As much as being received with such enthusiasm from the crowd made my job a pleasure, there was something great about having Ashley backstage tonight.

I loved looking out towards the wings of the stage and catching sight of the gorgeous Ashley waiting for me. Occasionally, she caught me looking at her and a wide smile would erupt on her luscious lips.

A warm, comforting feeling gurgled up inside of me.

"Eyes front," Murf growled from behind me. We were at one of the breaks between a mini set of songs. A chance for the band to check in with each other—even though we did that constantly throughout the show, these moments helped keep us tight.

Sam stood out front with Dusty doing their *I love her—she*

hates me—I'm the star—she's just a guitar player routine that every crowd we'd come across seemed to adore.

The key members of the band had their own little, well rehearsed, slot where they played up to the crowd. Entertainment, Julian had called it when he choreographed each piece with care and attention. We'd also discovered since we'd been out on the road that something about our British accents seemed to drive the crowds crazy.

My turn would come later, towards the end of the first set. As part of my set up, I recorded a session for the channel and then the fans voted on what they wanted me to do at the next show. It usually involved me taking my shirt off. Sam played cameraman for my segment and the rest of the band gave me shit. I remained pretty certain the only reason Julian had tolerated my escapades with the camera was because he and especially, Mags knew the power of internet marketing.

But for now, with Sam and Dusty entertaining front of house, Murf gave me more shit than usual.

"Any chance you can keep your head in the game and out of her panties," Murf joked, drum sticks sitting idly in one hand, while the other held a bottle of water.

It remained as hot as hell on stage. I could smell Ashley on my body. So could probably half the band, but I didn't give a fuck about that. I was proud that she wanted to be with me.

"Shut the fuck up," I snapped, I didn't want the band to think that they could treat Ashley anything like the way they generally treated the girls we picked up on the road.

Ashley meant something to me. I wasn't going to stand for any kind of shit from anyone.

"Testy," he said, one of his fold back plugs hanging from the top of his shirt. I was tempted to put mine back in so I didn't have to listen to him.

"She's not like the others," I said casting a quick glance in

Ashley's direction, "so stop being an arsehole." Mags, Julian's partner and Sam's almost sister-in-law stood at Ashley's side. She'd flown from her home in New Zealand to meet Julian. Originally they were to meet in New York, but because we were negotiating an extension of the tour, she'd come earlier. Their baby daughter was in the care of their travelling nanny. I couldn't imagine what it must be like trying to bring up a family, keep a band on the road and have anything that resembled a normal life. But somehow, Julian and Mags seemed to be doing it.

The poor woman used to keep Julian in line when he was on the road—pretty much the same way that Julian kept the rest of us in line now.

I couldn't decide whether or not it was a good thing for Mags to be talking to Ashley, but from the glimpses I'd caught of the two of them together, I could see, there was plenty of smiling going on, so they must have been getting on well.

"Point taken," Murf said stabbing a drum stick in my direction. "You like this one. I get it." He put his earpiece back in and ended the conversation.

I knew that he'd get the word to the other guys. Murf and I had been mates forever. Nothing about my life had ever been kept from him and neither his from me. Wordy explanations weren't needed. At least now I knew that the rest of the band would tone down their teasing once he spread the word.

We pumped our way through the balance of the set, the crowd were really digging the band and we were tight. We'd been on the road long enough that everyone knew what they were doing. There was nothing like touring to turn a rag-tag bunch of individual musicians into one live, breathtaking act.

Right on cue, Sam called me forward, for my turn to take centre stage.

I pulled out my earpiece and the deafening roar of the crowd washed over me. Next to sex with Ashley, this was the other thing that I lived for. Nothing could explain the feeling when the crowd were calling your name.

Demanding a piece of you.

They wanted me.

Stepping up there, I felt like I owned the fucking world.

One of the stage hands had placed a guitar stand to my left. I pulled the strap from my bass over my head and sat my Fender precision on the stand and then threw Sam my phone.

"So, what won the vote for tonight's show?" Sam asked. He knew full well what had won the vote, but we went through this routine every night.

"I gotta give the folks ten in the middle of the stage," I replied, readying myself to get down and do ten push-ups.

"Hey wait a minute," Sam said, "haven't you forgotten something?"

I pretended to think about it and then shook my head in the negative. "Nah, nothing," I said kneeling on the ground in front of him.

The crowd went wild.

I could see Dusty out of the corner of my eye mouthing words at them. I continued on, readying myself to assume a push-up position. The camera crew who were recording the show for the big screens moved in closer.

The roar of, "Strip! Strip! Strip!" Started from the crowd.

The word had by now been flashed up on the huge screens either side of the stage.

I leaned down on my hands, ready to start doing push ups. Dusty and the rest of the band cupped their ears, encouraging the crowd to shout louder.

"Hey! Hey!" Sam called, swinging his hand across in front of the crowd, demanding quiet.

The chanting fell away. An air of anticipation fell across the crowd. Sam's ability to control twenty thousand people with the single wave of his hand always left me in awe of what we'd created on this tour and in such a short amount of time.

I never wanted to give this up.

The power.

The control.

The incredible feeling of having twenty thousand people waiting on your next move.

It was more intoxicating than anything I'd ever experienced in my life.

The reason we got up here.

The reason we lived in metal cans on wheels and toured the country.

This moment.

The payoff.

I wasn't giving this up for anyone.

Sam winked at me, then addressed the crowd.

"What's he forgotten girls?"

I stood up and held my hands palm up and shrugged as if I had no idea what he was talking about.

The wall of sound engulfed us again.

"His shirt?" Sam played out the moment, talking direct to the crowd. Driving them to a frothing crescendo.

"Apparently you need to lose the shirt, pal," Sam said, throwing a casual arm around my shoulder.

"Really?"

Dusty arrived next to us, with a cellphone in her hand. "That's right," she said, her trademark Paul Reed Smith guitar hung from her front. The blue bird she had tattooed on her hip peaked out above the body of the guitar. I realised for the first time that the tattoo was the same as one of the birds on the fret board of her guitar.

"Eighty four percent voted in favour of you losing your shirt." Dusty turned to the crowd, "What do you say girls, does Paul need to lose the shirt before he gives us ten?"

More screaming from the crowd.

Griff started to play a sleazy sounding stripping song.

Carried by the enthusiasm of the crowd screaming for me, I waltzed across the front of the stage, making eye contact with a few of the girls out the front. Playing up. Milking the moment for what it was worth.

The crowd were eating out of our hands.

By the time I got down to do the push ups, my adrenaline levels were so high I could easily have pushed out sixty. But the script called for ten and I'd keep to the script.

---

*A*shley

    I couldn't believe what I was seeing.

The show had evolved since Vegas. I'd been watching Paul's channel and I'd seen the numerous clips of him doing similar routines to this one, but I didn't expect to feel anything like this.

An intense an overwhelming wave of jealousy hit me like a truck.

Mags put a hand on my arm.

I turned to face her and a look of concern crossed her features. "You'll get used to it," she said.

"Really?" My voice sounded too strained and too short even to me.

She nodded. "Yes, really. It's his job. It doesn't mean anything to him." I couldn't be sure.

"He seems to be enjoying it," I heard myself say.

Mags laughed, throwing back her long, dark hair. "Of

course he's enjoying it. None of them would be out there if being in the limelight didn't do something for them."

"Why are you here?" I asked. "On the road when you could be home with your baby."

"Because Julian loves being on the road and I love Jules." She shrugged. "He likes being at home when we're at home, but this is where he really shines. It's what he's really about. I watch him when he gets up on stage and sings that portion of the set with Sam. It's who they are. It's what they are. I couldn't imagine ever suggesting to Jules that he give up his music or give up being on the road. He might cut back from it for a while. Well, he's done that. When Annabelle was born he stepped back. Away completely from touring. But now that Sam's on the road." She laughed, "Sam was supposed to be a vehicle for Julian's music, so Jules could stay at home with me and Annabelle but it's not quite worked out that way."

"And you're not bitter about that?" I imagined I would be pissed. I was trying not to compare me and Paul to Julian and Mags, but seeing them on the road, with a baby, I couldn't help but let my mind go in that direction.

"No," a warm smile spread across her face. "You know, I think I might have been at the outset. But the more I see the two of them on stage, the more I think that it would just suck the life out of Jules if he thought he could never tour again."

I tried to put it all into perspective in my own head. "So, you'll come here. From the other side of the world and follow them on the road."

Mags nodded. "Yeah. I don't want to be doing it every day of my life. We can avoid the northern winter back home. It's winter there now, so I get to enjoy a northern summer."

"Wow."

"Don't get me wrong, where we live, we're not knee deep in snow or anything." A wistful look crossed her face. "In fact we don't get any snow at all, which is a blessing. After all those years I lived in London, I wouldn't cross the street for snow. I love the sub-tropical lifestyle in New Zealand, but it can still get cold and wet in winter. Even if the sun does come out every day."

"I can't imagine it," I said, "We get so much rain here and I couldn't stand it down the coast. Vegas nearly killed me with the heat."

Mags laughed, "It's nothing like the heat of Vegas. It's nice. And we have the pool and Jules spends most of his time in the air-conditioned studio writing, anyway."

The more I spoke to Mags the more I could see that there were so many complex layers to the man that I'd just watched flex his inked and muscled body in front of twenty thousand people.

He'd put his shirt back on and taken his place back on stage just in front of the drummer.

Paul turned and caught my eye and winked at me.

The flush of heat that spread through my body extended up to my face.

Mags leaned in and said, "You're caught in his trap. Take my advice. Don't fight it. You can spend a long time tying yourself up in knots over a guy like Paul and there's no shortage of women throwing themselves at him."

Even in the short time that I'd been in Vegas, I'd watched the fans throwing themselves at band members. Hell, I lived with a woman who'd taken it upon herself to try to bed as many musicians in a year as she could.

I didn't have Madi's drive to behave like that, but I could see from the women stood in front of the stage tonight that she wasn't alone in her groupie obsession.

My hand fell instinctively to my stomach and the new life that grew inside of me. "But how do you know that it's going to work out?" I asked Mags.

"Because he chose me." She said. "Because he comes home to me. Because I'm the stability in his life." She waved her hand out in front of the stage. "All of this. It can go in an instant. But he knows that I'll aways be there for him and that's why it works."

I wanted to believe her. I really did. But I still couldn't get the image of a half naked Paul doing press ups in front of twenty thousand screaming fans from my mind.

Why would he choose a puking, pregnant me over that?

CHAPTER 9

*P*aul

Since Mags had joined us, a blanket of decent behaviour had washed across the tour. She brought something with her. An edge of respectability that we might have been missing up until she arrived.

I guess having the baby here meant that a few more of us were watching our general conduct.

Beside that, something had changed with Ashley since I'd been on stage and I wasn't sure what that could be.

"What a fucking brilliant show," Julian said, "one of the best yet."

"We brought the house down," Sam added. "Paul, you were fucking amazing. They love you." I felt Ashley stiffen beside me at the mention of my stint out the front of the stage.

Julian said, "Three encores is nothing to be sniffed at." He slapped his brother hard on the back, "And the best set yet with my bro here on stage."

I'd watched the relationship between the two brothers blossom on the road. It was clear at the outset of the tour that Sam had been Julian's junior, but as we'd played night after night, Sam had found his groove. It wasn't just that the crowds had warmed to him, but also that he'd grown into the role of a rockstar. Not only was there a maturity about our performance as a cohesive band, but also Sam's performance as front man.

Mags and Julian had decided that the entire band should stay away from the city after the show.

"You're not getting out in amongst it tonight," Julian said in that tone of voice we'd all grown to know meant business. "But," he added, throwing us a bone, "You can have a leave pass after the final show."

He'd arranged for catering to bring a meal for everyone backstage. We all sat around, poking shit at each other and enjoying a few after show beverages.

"What can I get you to drink?" I asked Ashley. "There's wine, or beer, or champagne." Mags barely drank herself, but she always made sure that there was plenty on hand for the crew after a show.

"A soft drink will be fine," Ashley said.

"Great." I knocked the top off a bottle of beer for me and found Ashley a can of juice. I liked that she didn't want to get hammered—it was a welcome change after some of the girls that had been around on this tour. Some of the guys were hitting it a little harder than I'd want to on a work night—but that was none of my business. I'd done enough heavy drinking after shows in my time.

Despite the amount of alcohol and food consumed, the guys had settled somewhat. Mercifully, I wasn't on the end of the ribbing that was doing the rounds of the room. I wasn't sure whether it was the sobering influence of Mags and Julian and Sam and Dusty, or whether Murf had spread the word already—but everyone seemed somewhat restrained around me and Ashley.

While we ate, the banter and bullshit flew back and forth across the table, but Ashley seemed quiet. Distracted almost. I worried about what Mags had said to her while they stood in the wings.

"You ready to head back?" I slipped my hand onto Ashley's under the table and gave it a reassuring squeeze.

"Yes," she nodded, "I need to pick up my pack and then catch my train."

Train.

Fuck that.

There was no question of Ashley getting on a train tonight. Not at this hour. I kept my mouth shut and let her say a round of goodbyes, but there was no way she was going to be leaving my van once we got there.

I'd make sure of that.

We got back to the van and Ashley went to my room to get her bag. I followed her and then closed the door behind us, putting me clearly between her and the exit.

"You're not going home at this time of the night," I said.

Ashley pulled her pack onto her back. "I'll come back and see you tomorrow."

"What's wrong?"

"Nothing," she said almost too quickly.

"Bullshit!" I could stand a lot of things, but lies weren't one of them. "You've been quiet ever since the show. What's up?"

"Look. You're tired. I need to get the last train and we can talk about this tomorrow." Ashley's dark brown eyes stared straight into mine. "Please let me get past."

"You're not going anywhere until we have this out," I said crossing my arms and refusing to move. "So you may as well take off your pack and sit your pretty little arse back down on the bed and tell me what's going on."

82

Ashley licked her lips and then straightened her shoulders. "Paul, get out of my way."

"Make me," I said.

She slipped the strap of her pack over the other shoulder, got a good grip of my arms and pulled.

Hard.

She was surprisingly strong, but no matter how hard she pulled, or pushed, Ashley couldn't move me from in front of the door. I watched with fascination and then increasing concern as her attempts to move me failed.

Eventually, in total frustration she sat down on the bed. Eyes filling with tears. "Paul, just get out of the way and let me go home."

"No," I said, "you're upset. Tell me what's the matter."

"I'm pregnant," she whispered.

At first the word didn't register.

"Pregnant?"

She nodded. Tears streaming down her face.

"Is it mine?"

In an instant she turned on me, like a snake.

"Of course it's fucking yours. Who else could it be?"

I opened my mouth to say that I had no idea. Then I thought better of it and kept my mouth shut. She could have had a boyfriend. I knew nothing about Ashley's life. I wanted to know more, but there had only really been that one night in Vegas.

One night.

Pregnant.

Fuck.

"Are you sure?"

"Of course I'm fucking sure!" She screamed back at me as she stood up, thew her back pack on the bed and began to pace the tiny space between us.

"Okay, okay." Maybe I should have let her out of the room

when I had a chance. An explosive Ashley wasn't something that I'd had the chance to experience before.

Then it dawned on me. "You've been here all this time. We've—"

"I know," she said a stricken look on her face. "I didn't mean that to happen before. But you kissed me and..." She sat down on the bed, like a deflated balloon, it was as if all the fight had suddenly gone from her body. She crossed her arms and kind of folded in on herself.

Pregnant.

Fuck.

I couldn't get my head around the concept. I'd been watching Mags and Julian with Annabelle. I didn't know how he managed it. Being a father.

Fuck.

I was going to be a father.

I sat down next to Ashley.

"We can work something out," I said. I wasn't ready to be a father.

"We can?" She sniffed, turning to look at me, her eyelashes dark with unshed tears.

"Of course we can," I said sounding more sure of myself then I felt.

"Stay here with me tonight," I said pulling the tight ball of her body into mine. Ashley's began to relax against mine. I could feel the tension slowly releasing itself from her body.

"I'm sorry," she snivelled.

"Hey," I said trying to sound upbeat, "you didn't do this by yourself."

"But I thought we'd been so careful," she said the words muffled against my chest. "I've been over everything in my head so many times."

I could easily have said, 'me too,' but I'd been over the

entire night we spent together in Vegas for completely different reasons.

In fact, the idea of sex this minute had gone right out of my mind. All I wanted to do was hold Ashley and try to make her feel better.

"Look," I said, "we're both tired. How about we get some sleep and then we can talk about this in the morning?"

"Okay," she said, "you win. I'll stay the night."

I didn't know if you could describe it as winning and it certainly wasn't the way that I'd planned to spend the night.

I woke and Ashley was nowhere to be seen.

Strange gagging noises seemed to be coming from somewhere. I found a pair of shorts, threw them on and headed out into the main part of the van. It was coming from the bathroom.

"Can you shut her up?" Murf moaned from the bed in the corner. "How much did she drink last night?"

"What do you mean?" I asked.

"Your bird, Ashley, she's been in there puking her ring up for nearly half an hour."

Shit.

I tapped on the door, "Ashley, it's me, Paul are you okay?"

"I will be in a minute," the muffled reply came from through the door.

No wonder she wanted to go home last night. I knew she'd had nothing to drink, but thankfully, no-one else did.

"Can I get you a drink?" I called through the door.

"I think she had enough last night," Murf moaned from the bed before turning over and burying his head under his pillow.

The door opened and a pale Ashley stood in front of me.

"Water would be good," she said. Dark rings sat under her eyes. I don't think I'd seen her looking this unwell before.

Then I remembered. How could I have forgotten?

She was pregnant.

The thought lay heavy on me.

All of a sudden, the van seemed too small. I had a need to step outside.

I had a sudden sense of how a fox must feel when it was surrounded by yapping dogs.

Trapped.

Ashley headed back towards my room and I followed as soon as I could find a clean glass to fill with water.

My hand shook when I gave it to her.

"Thank you," she said.

Sitting on the bed, taking small sips of water, she looked fragile and broken.

"Is this how it is every morning?" I asked.

She nodded, "Yes. It's the reason I've lost my job. I can't do anything until lunchtime and the vomiting stops."

"Shouldn't you see a doctor?"

"I have seen a doctor," she snapped.

Anger welled inside of me. I began to pace the tiny space. I hadn't signed on for this. Yes, I liked Ashley enough, but I was on tour. I didn't need this kind of shit.

I had an obligation to the band.

I had a channel.

I had fans who needed me.

We were on the cusp of creating something amazing and now this.

"How much do you need?" I asked.

"What?" Ashley replied.

"Money." I said, "How much money do you need to sort this out."

"W-what do you mean, sort it out?" Ashley asked. Then

she stood up, her nostrils flaring. "You think I came here and slept with you yesterday because I'm looking for money?"

"No." I held my hands up, palms facing Ashley, trying to calm her down. I should have held her, but ever since she'd told me about the pregnancy it was as if something stood between us. Every time I went to move towards her, some invisible force stopped me getting close. Touching her.

What did I mean? Why was I offering her money?

You want this to go away.

The thought came from some deep and primordial part of my brain.

But I didn't want Ashley to go away.

Somehow the two things were inextricably linked together and I didn't know how to tear them apart, without tearing Ashley apart.

"Because if that's what you think," Ashley said anger raging through her as she stormed around the tiny space, putting on her jeans and zipping up her bag.

Then she stopped dead.

Threw her hand over her mouth and rushed out of the room.

I sat down on the bed.

It was then I realised that we hadn't even gotten undressed properly last night. We'd slept in my bed, both of us wearing underwear and t-shirts.

We'd already become some kind of married couple. Tied to each other by the obligation of a baby.

A fucking baby!

Shit!

I buried my head in my hands. What the fuck was I going to do now?

CHAPTER 10

*a*shley

I wasn't staying a moment longer than necessary.

What the hell I thought I'd achieve by coming here and telling Paul that I was pregnant I didn't know. He had the fucking cheek to offer me money. Probably so that I'd go and have an abortion. He didn't need to say the word. But the inference was there. He didn't want this interfering with his happy little touring life. He didn't need to say that either, it was perfectly clear.

He'd not laid a hand on me since he'd found out I was pregnant.

Or that's how it felt to me.

I didn't care if I ended up puking on the train, I was leaving and that was the end of it. I stormed back to the small space that I'd been occupying with Paul, oblivious to anyone who might be around me. I had one thing on my mind and it was getting out of this trailer and getting back home.

A red hot rage drove me and I wasn't going to let anything or anyone get in my way. Least of all the man who I thought could help me through this.

I could feel the tears welling in my eyes. I'd been stupid coming here.

All I'd done was end up back in Paul's bed and, before he found out about the baby that had seemed like a good place to be.

But now.

I shuddered at my stupidity. My naivete. Why did I think a rockstar who could have anyone in the world would want a pregnant me?

A flush of humiliation ran through my body.

This wasn't how I'd planned my life.

All my college plans had been dashed.

Maybe Maddi was right. Maybe…

I couldn't even go there.

I would go away. I would have this baby and then I would get back on with the plans I had for the rest of my life. I wasn't the first woman in the world who had her plan put on hold because of a life growing inside of her and I certainly wasn't going to be the last.

There.

I'd made a decision.

Somehow I felt better.

For some reason, the churning in my gut settled.

Maybe that was all I needed to do. Make a decision.

I'd go home to my Mom and Dad. They'd be shocked, but in the end they'd understand. I knew they would support my decision. They would never countenance me having an abortion.

Shit, I could barely event think about the word.

They might be unhappy that I hadn't done things quite in the order that they would have liked, but we'd get through this. Together.

"You're not leaving?" Paul's words didn't have the authority that they'd had last night. More importantly, this morning in the clear light of day, after I'd finally come to terms with my situation, they didn't have any sway on me.

"I'm going home and you can't stop me."

"But we need to talk."

He didn't sound convinced.

"Look, Paul," I said as I stared into that one single, piercing blue eye, "I don't know what you're doing with your life, but I'm having this baby."

There, I'd said the words. Somehow I felt better.

"You don't get to make that decision on your own."

"It's my body and I get to decide what happens to it and the life that's growing inside of it." He'd woven some kind of strange spell over me. Being here in this room with him. From the very first night in Vegas it was as if my brain had malfunctioned. Gone into under drive. I'd had some kind of metaphysical frontal lobotomy as soon as I set foot in the trailer.

It must have something to do with the hypnotic way he moved on stage. Or, I shuddered as I thought about it, the way my body reacted to his touch, his taste, his smell.

Well. He'd barely touched me in the last twelve hours or so and that was all I needed to come to my senses.

"Baby," he reached out to touch me and then hesitated again.

I scowled at him, "Look at you. You can't even touch me now that you know I'm pregnant. I can see that the idea of a baby disgusts you. So I won't bother you with it anymore."

I pulled my bag on my back.

"You can't go, there are things we have to talk about. To work out." He ran his fingers through the long mop of his hair. One side fell across his eye. The look he gave me reminded me of the first time I saw him at the gate in Vegas.

That same tremble fluttered in my stomach.

I needed to get out of here.

Before I lost my nerve.

"You can email me," I said as I turned my back on him.

"Can't we at least talk about this," Paul followed me out of the room.

"Lovebirds having a tiff," Murf said from under the blankets.

"Fuck up!" Paul said.

I was out the door and in the carpark before Paul caught up to me. He grabbed my arm and swung me around to face him. That one blue eye staring at me with what?

"You're not going anywhere until we discuss what we're doing about this."

Fury boiled over inside of me. I wrenched my arm from his grasp. "We're not discussing anything!" I gritted my teeth. I would not throw up. "There's nothing to discuss."

"I can't be a father," he whispered. "Look at my life. I'm on the road, with a band. You can't do this to me."

"It's not all about you," I snapped. My life had been turned upside down and inside out and all he could think about was the band and his life.

I turned on my heel and walked towards the stadium exit. I wasn't going to stay here for another moment. I'd made my decision and now I knew where I was heading.

I didn't need Paul Gray and neither did my baby.

---

*P*aul

    I watched Ashley walk away and thought about trying to stop her, but something inside of me prevented me from calling out.

Selfishness?

Fear?

Anger?

I couldn't be sure. But by the time I decided it might be a good idea to try to stop her, she'd turned a corner and I knew she'd be out on the street before I had a chance to catch up.

I stormed back to the van. Unsure of what to do next, I headed for my room.

"Lovebirds are having a tiff," Murf said as I walked by.

I ignored him. He could think what he wanted to think. I needed some time to get my head around what Ashley had just said to me.

She wanted to keep this baby.

The idea made me want to rush into the bathroom and vomit.

No wonder she spent the morning puking. And she'd had some time to get her head around the idea.

I started trying to put together how long we'd been on the road. How far she must be into the pregnancy. How many weeks I had left to try to convince her that she should let me pay to make this problem go away.

There was a knock on the door, Murf's voice. "What's up mate."

"Nothing, leave me alone."

He ignored me and opened the door. Stood there looking at me. He tipped his head sideways and said, "Trouble at mill?"

"I don't want to talk about it."

"You know I can keep my mouth shut," he said as he came inside and closed the door behind him.

Murf always looked out of place in the confined spaces where we slept. He brought a powerful presence to the tiny room. The man mountain who sat behind the drums still somehow didn't seem out of place when he wanted to play agony aunt.

"She's pregnant." I closed my eyes and let out a long breath. I think it was the first time that I'd actually said the word. Somehow it felt as if my lips stumbled over it. The syllables sticking to the roof of my mouth. I'd avoided saying the word, as if vocalising it somehow gave the situation more power.

"Fuck," He let a breath out, "no wonder she was puking her ring out this morning." Murf shook his head, "and I thought she just got on the piss last night and couldn't handle it."

I snorted. "I wish." I threw myself back against the pillows on the bed. "She's got some insane idea that she wants to keep it."

"Ouch."

"Ouch is a fucking understatement." I said, as I closed my eyes. Maybe I could go to sleep, wake up and this would all be some kind of horrible dream.

No. Wait. I tried that last night and the reality still hung around this morning, even if Ashley had done a runner on me.

"You offered to take care of it?" Murf asked, "you know, get her to the best clinic."

I nodded, "Yeah. Why the fuck do you think she's taken off this morning. Says she doesn't want to take my stinking money. Or words to that effect." I threw my arms wide, "I mean, I can't be a father. Fucking look at me."

"I know, mate, I know." Murf said, nodding in agreement. "It's no life for a baby on the road. I don't know how the fuck Julian does it."

"He's got Mags. She's brilliant." I said.

"Plus the nanny," Murf added.

"And the billions in the bank."

"There is that," he agreed.

"I mean," I said not sure who I was trying to convince, me or Murf, "we're going to make it."

"If we stick with Sam and Julian," Murf added.

"Exactly," I said. "But fuck only knows what will happen with me or the channel if I give up touring. I mean what am I going to share?" I sat up on the bed, now that I was thinking it through. "Oh look, the baby's sitting up, or eating its first solids, or walking." I shook my head. "I mean, who's going to tune in for that?"

Murf nodded in agreement, "Yeah, especially after this tour. Are they going to vote on which nappy you should change, or whether or not you should bottle feed today?"

It all sounded ridiculous to me. I could feel the edge of impending doom creeping up on me.

"It would never work," I said. "All our work down the tubes."

"You sure it's yours?" Murf asked, "you could get a paternity test. You know what these girls are like on the road. They'll fucking tell you anything if there's a chance that they can make it more than a one night thing."

I had a sudden rush of protective feelings for Ashley. "She doesn't sleep around," I snapped.

Murf held up his hands in surrender. "Hey, don't shoot the messenger."

"I'm sorry," I muttered, "I'm not thinking straight."

Murf lifted his chin in acknowledgment of the apology. "No skin off my nose, pal. But what would Robbie do?"

"Fuck off with Robbie Williams." Murf had worshipped Robbie ever since I'd known him. Most would say *What would Jesus do*. But not Murf, he was all about Robbie.

"Think about it." Murf pulled the ear buds out of his phone, swiped his hands across the screen and all of a sudden the tiny space filled with the intro for *Angels*.

I watched as a look of intense, what? Could it be described as pleasure, or contentment crossed Murf's features.

"Oh, fuck, no," I moaned.

He opened his eyes, "Just listen."

I'd heard the song a thousand times. Not just because Murf played it, but because it had become a classic British ballad. But this time, I heard something different. I heard a promise that no matter what happened in my life—no matter which way it went—that things would be okay.

Maybe that was what Murf wanted me to hear this morning. I didn't know. But what I did know was that music had been my own personal mistress for so many years. I wasn't about to give her up for anyone or anything.

But, I knew I had to take responsibility for what had happened between me and Ashley.

Somehow I had to find a way to make things right.

I had no idea how I was going to do that today.

But, strangely, Murf and Robbie had shone a light and shown me the way.

CHAPTER 11

*a*shley
     I sat on the train heading home.

It wasn't so much that Paul had offered me money that offended me as the fact that as soon as he found out I was pregnant he'd been repelled by me. Treated me like I had some kind of communicable disease. Truth be told if it wasn't for him I wouldn't be in this position.

A tiny logical voice in my head—the one I didn't want to listen to—whispered that maybe he and Madi might be right. I didn't want to contemplate that idea.

I reminded myself that I was the person who couldn't bear to kill even an insect. As long as I could remember, I would be the one who would usher all kinds of critters out of the house. Even now, in the apartment with Madi, as much as I hated cockroaches, I still couldn't bring myself to kill them.

How could I even countenance taking money from Paul? To what? Get rid of me and the problem that I'd become.

I could feel the tears trickling down my face and I swiped them away in frustration.

I would not cry.

He would not have that kind of power over me.

I was a grown woman. I had resources and I didn't need him, or his money.

Anger rose inside of me.

What was I thinking? Going to him?

The thought of his hands all over me. The way the calloused tips of his fingers felt as they drifted across my skin. The intense way he looked at me. The tiny sounds of pleasure coming from him when we made love.

A flush of heat ran through my body at the memory.

These were things that I couldn't get out of my mind, no matter how angry I was with him now.

It's just the shock. Another tiny voice in my head said to me. He'll come round. Give him time.

I didn't know whether I wanted him to come round. Or whether I wanted to give him time.

What kind of a life could he offer me and a baby, anyway? He was on the road every minute of every day.

No.

I'd come up with a plan.

I was on my way home to tell Madi that I would be moving back in with my parents.

My parents!

I had to tell Mom and Dad. Ever since I'd made the decision to move back home and find some support with them, the overwhelming feelings of nausea had left me.

Now, the harsh reality had hit. I was going to do it and I was going to have to tell them that their perfect daughter had made a complete mess of her life.

The nausea washed over me again, replacing the sense of wellbeing. A tiny part of me wished that Paul sat beside me. That I could take him to break the news to my parents. But that would never happen. He'd made that clear, the way he'd responded to me.

My cell phone vibrated in my pocket.

A text from Paul.

"We need to talk."

All I wanted to do was run away from him. Yet, I knew he had a say in what I did going forward.

"There's nothing to say." I texted back.

"Bullshit." Another text followed the single word. "You can't run away."

"You don't know where I live."

"Won't take Otis long to find you."

Was he kidding?

"You can run, but you can't hide :)"

As pissed off as I was with him the smilie face made me grin.

"I can try."

"I will hunt you down!"

A warm feeling began to grow inside of me again. Something about the man had intrigued me from the moment that I looked into that single blue eye.

"Come back...."

I didn't want to go back, but I still found Paul totally irresistible, despite my anger at his suggestion that his money would fix everything.

"I'm still pissed at you." I texted back

"Understood."

"We can't talk in the trailer."

"How about your place?"

The idea of Paul in the tiny space that Madi and I occupied didn't thrill me. As an aside, Madi would likely tear the balls off him if given a chance.

"No."

I arrived at my train stop and got off the train. The day

had become overcast and rain threatened. Not unusual for this time of the year. The weather reflected my mood. Thin strips of weak sunshine trying to break through rolling dark clouds.

"I'll book a hotel for the next two nights. Meet me there?"

That seemed like a compromise. We'd have a chance to be alone and discuss a way forward.

"Okay." I replied.

The first smatterings of rain began to fall. I pulled the hood of my sweat up over my head and tried to stay under the shop awnings as I made my way back to our apartment.

"Will text details soon x"

A kiss. I fixated on that tiny cross as I walked the rest of the way to the apartment. The rent was due soon and I'd have my last pay packet coming, but after that I had no idea where the money would come from.

He's offering you money.

I tried to ignore the rogue thought.

No matter what happened. I wasn't going to be taking Paul Gray's money and that was the end of it.

I pushed the door of the apartment open and congratulated myself on not agreeing to Paul coming here. The place looked as if a small ramshackle army had been through it. I'd been too sick to pick up after myself and Madi's idea of cleaning was putting the take out boxes in the trash at least once a week.

In fact, we would both have fit in quite easily on tour.

What the hell was I thinking, bringing a baby into something like this? My life was a complete disaster.

Madi looked up from the table, her red hair piled in a messy bun on the top of her head. What looked like a chopstick holding the pile precariously in place.

"I wasn't expecting you back until the band left Seattle."

"Surprise!" I said throwing my arms wide.

She eyed me with suspicion, "What happened?"

"He offered me money to get rid of the problem?"

"The problem being you or the baby?"

I shrugged. I liked to think that the problem was the baby and I held onto the tiny little kiss that he'd put on the end of his last text.

"I'm not sure."

"Bastard." Madi muttered. "How much did he offer you?"

I couldn't believe what I was hearing and threw Madi what I hoped was a death stare.

"A girl can ask," she said. "You know the rent's due next week and you haven't got a job?"

"You don't have to sound so mercenary about it."

"Just pointing out the facts," Madi said.

"I don't need help with the facts," I said as I washed out a mug and looked for a teabag in the pantry. I would have had to be blind to see that there was next to nothing in the cupboard to eat. Madi lived on takeout and I had eaten nothing but breakfast cereal for the last week.

My phone vibrated and I pulled it out of my jacket.

"It's him, isn't it?" Madi asked.

I nodded.

"W booked under the name Peter Williams. Get there ASAP."

"What does he want?"

I ignored the question and sent a text back saying, "ok."

The jug boiled and I poured hot water on the tea bag. I checked the fridge for milk. Found a carton and took off the lid. "How long's this been here?" I screwed up my nose as the acrid scent of stale milk hit me.

"Who knows," Madi said. "What does the bastard want?"

"Don't call him that."

"Okay," she rolled her eyes, "What does Paul want?"

"He wants me to meet him at the W."

"Fuck! He's got money to burn. Are you going?"

"Yes. We need to sort a few things out."

"Don't suppose you're going to the show again tonight and you can get me backstage?" Madi asked, an evil grin on her face.

"No and no. I can't believe you'd ask me that after what I've been through."

Madi shrugged. "They're a hot band. I thought I'd catch up with Todd again."

"It was your obsession with rock stars that's gotten me into this mess."

"You can't blame this on me," Madi said with a smile.

As much as I didn't want to hear that, I knew she was telling me the truth. Madi hadn't forced me into Paul's trailer and he hadn't held a gun to my head and insisted that I sleep with him.

I'd gotten myself into this little mess all by myself and now I had to find a way out.

I arrived at the hotel less than an hour after I'd gotten the text from Paul.

A striking building in the middle of town. The kind of hotel that I'd never be able to afford to stay in, with its spacious interior and its amazing artwork. The staff had a hip, but refined edge to them. I had a sense of immediately being out of place and wondered again why I'd agreed to Paul's request.

Then my hand fluttered to my stomach and I knew I had my answer. I would do whatever was needed to make sure that this child growing inside of me had a secure future. If that meant traipsing all over the city to meet with a man who had an ego the size of the entranceway to this hotel, then so be it.

The concierge eyed me with suspicion from behind a large walnut desk that stood in front of a wall of bright, modern artwork. He was nothing like the crusty kind of concierge that I expected would work in a hotel like this. He could easily have been on tour with the boys, with the line of tattoos up his arms and his thick, reddish brown beard. Still, I couldn't shake the feeling that his subtle smile hid a smirk when he handed me a plastic swipe card and called me, *Mrs Williams*.

"Now, Mrs Williams," he coughed and I shuffled my feet. "Do you have any luggage for us to take to the suite?"

I could feel the heat racing up my face.

Suite.

Paul had booked a freaking suite. Why couldn't he book a room like a normal person? Oh, wait a minute, he was a rockstar. It seemed that everything they did had to be on a large scale.

"No," I replied trying to keep the squeak out of my voice. I'd come straight from the apartment and was now acutely aware of the small pack I carried on my back. The same one I'd carried with me to the show the night before. This time, though, I'd thrown in a couple of changes of clothes. The pack still didn't constitute luggage in terms of the kind of luggage a hotel guest would bring with them to stay in a suite.

"Fine," the concierge said and with a small nod of the head, another staff member appeared out of nowhere by my side. "Gareth will accompany you upstairs and settle you into the suite." He handed Gareth another plastic card that looked like a duplicate of the one I'd been given and we were on our way.

Gareth could have been the concierge's twin, except he sported hair that had been dyed a fascinating shade of platinum—a startling contrast to the well groomed, dark hair of his beard.

As Gareth and I stood in the elevator in silence making our way to the top floor of the hotel, I wondered who made the booking and ordered a suite of rooms. I didn't think that it would have been Paul. From what I had observed in the short time I had been around the band, they all seemed to have a team of people who looked after their every need. Paul's only job was to make sure that he performed well on stage. I guess it was a matter of making sure that he kept his mind on that.

I knew I must be a terrible distraction.

I wondered whether or not the rest of the band knew what was going on. I certainly wouldn't be going backstage for the show tonight. The idea of any one of them looking at me the way that the concierge had looked at me brought on that ever familiar feeling of nausea.

The lift came to an almost silent halt and the doors opened.

Gareth slipped the thin plastic card into a holder by the side of the elevator door and the space in front of me came alive with subdued lighting.

I'd never seen anything like it.

Gareth stood to one side, his arm in front of the doors, encouraging me to exit the elevator.

I felt like Alice stepping into wonderland.

The entranceway could easily have accommodated half of the apartment that Madi and I lived in. Beyond the marble floor and the elegant statues in white and gold that adorned the entranceway lay part of the suite itself.

"Ms Williams, may I take your bag?" Gareth asked, holding out his hand, an expectant look in his face.

Feeling the heat rush to my face again, I went to open my mouth and correct him, but then I thought better of it. Paul had chosen this name for a reason. No doubt so that he wouldn't be recognised. It seemed odd to me. Having to hide your identity. Nobody cared who I was, but then I guess I'd been careful to make sure that my image wasn't plastered all over the internet for the entire world to consume. I shrugged the canvas pack off my back and handed it to Gareth.

The sincere smile that crossed his even features calmed my frazzled nerves.

"I'll place this in the bedroom for you," Gareth said, "please follow me." There was nothing about the way he said the words, or the way he treated me, that I could complain about. But still, I could feel the disapproval oozing from him. Or was that my imagination? Why would any of the staff have any contempt for me? The suite had been paid for by someone, so maybe I should stop caring about what the staff might think about me.

But for some reason, I found that particularly difficult.

As I followed Gareth through numerous rooms, I realised that this suite on the top floor of the hotel could have accommodated the entire floor in my building.

Twenty people could be ushered in this space and no-one would be in the way of anyone else.

Gareth lay my pathetic looking pack on a large luggage rack at one side of the opulent bedroom.

"The bathroom is to the right," he said pointing toward what looked like a room containing nothing but glass and marble. "And the kitchen has been fully stocked with every-thing that Mr Williams asked for."

"Thank you," I said wondering what I was supposed to do now.

"I'll leave you to settle in," Gareth said as he made his way back towards the bedroom door. "Please feel free to contact reception if there is anything else that you need."

"Thank you," I said. I wasn't sure what else I might need. Paul seemed to have everything covered.

"Enjoy your stay with us, Ms Williams," Gareth said and with a nod of the head he was gone.

I couldn't imagine what he must have thought.

As I walked through the suite, taking in the plush interior. The furniture, which even I knew to be designer furniture and the funky and opulent colour scheme, it occurred to me that Paul had spared no expense.

I pondered the situation as I stood in front of the floor to ceiling window that gave me a panoramic view of the city beyond. I felt as if I were stood atop the clouds themselves.

Why weren't the band staying here? They were successful. Surely they could afford to accommodate themselves here in this kind of luxury instead of camping out in their vans at the venue.

"Do you like the view?"

Startled, at the sound of Paul's voice, I turned around and caught my breath at the sight of him.

The muscled torso, barely hidden under the tight t-shirt. Ink coming down his arms. The large gold signet ring that he wore, the one that caught the light when he played on stage, drawing my eye immediately to his long, strong fingers. Fingers that not only played his guitar, but also played a beautiful melody across my body.

I swallowed.

The sense of overwhelm threatening to take charge of my body.

No matter what, I needed to keep my whits about me. But I found that increasingly difficult in the presence of this powerful man. It made sense to me now, the number of followers he had on his internet channel. The way the band had charged up the charts. The way they had all taken America by storm.

Paul was a part of something that I didn't really under-stand. All I knew right now was that whenever he entered the room, I was powerless.

If the sound of his voice and the mere presence of him in the room could do this to me, what hope could I possibly have of brokering any kind of sensible deal with the man?

I turned into one of his simpering fans the moment that I set eyes on him.

"You didn't have to go to all this trouble," I said trying to look away from him. Turn back toward the view, but there was something about the way that he held me in his gaze. The way his hair fell across his face. The intense blue of that single eye as it tracked me across the room.

Who was I kidding?

I vacillated between wanting to throw my arms around his neck and rub myself against him like a cat and running in the other direction.

"It's no trouble," he replied, "and you haven't answered my question."

"The view's fantastic," I smiled at him. Only I don't think I was talking about the cityscape behind my back any longer.

As if he sensed my inability to think in his presence, Paul abruptly turned his back on me, making his way across to the small kitchen.

"Cup of tea?" he asked.

I couldn't help but laugh.

"You British, you think a cup of tea will solve everything," I snorted.

The warmth that lit his face as he acknowledged my words could have easily have been my undoing all over again.

"It does," He replied, "A cup of tea and a biscuit will solve the problems of the world."

"But will it solve our problem?" I asked, being brazen.

He put the jug on the hotplate and took his time to ensure that the correct hotplate had lit before he turned his attention back to me. When he did, he leaned across the counter and brushed the hair out of his eyes, so he could look at me with both of them.

Something about looking into both of his eyes brought home the seriousness of the situation.

The silence hung heavy in the room. The ornate furnishings and the bright colours of the designer furniture that I'd found so attractive when I walked in suddenly became overbearing and oppressive as the long silence dragged on.

Then Paul said in an earnest tone, "You and I can solve our problems, but you have to stop running away from me. You've got to let me in."

I wasn't so sure about letting Paul in. Letting him in had gotten me into this mess. How would letting him in further solve things for me or between us?

CHAPTER 12

*P*aul

The sound of the kettle boiling was enough to distract me from Ashley.

I'd brought her here because I wanted a chance to try to make things right. I didn't know how the hell I was going to make things right, but I knew that I needed a chance.

"Thank you for coming," I said as I poured us both a cup of tea.

"I realise that we need to talk," Ashley said as she looked at those long nails of hers. Nails that I'd enjoyed scraping down my back. Nails that I suddenly realised may have been responsible for the current situation we found ourselves in. She put the condom on. A little voice in my head said. No wonder she's pregnant. I told the voice to shut up. It was too late to lay blame, if that was the reason that she was pregnant, then I had some responsibility too. I was there.

I handed Ashley a cup of tea. No matter the situation we found ourselves in, I still wanted her. I wanted her like I'd never wanted another woman.

Something about the way she remained totally unaffected

by my fame. The way she treated me like I was just another bloke on the street. I liked it. It was refreshing and incredibly alluring.

But I could never ask Ashley to come on the road. Why would she want to join the circus that I called my life? Yet, I couldn't see me doing anything else.

Ours was a match where I couldn't see a future.

Ashley blew on the cup of tea, making tiny ripples on the liquid surface. I couldn't keep my eyes away from her lips and the memory of them sat snug around my cock.

"Can we start again?" I asked, taking a sip of the scalding liquid from my own cup.

She cocked her head to one side, "What do you mean, you haven't forgotten that I'm pregnant?"

I nearly choked on my next mouthful of tea.

"No, I've not forgotten," I replied, "But I'd like for you to agree to spend the next forty-eight hours here with me."

"You've got shows."

I nodded. "I know, but I only have to go and do the shows. I'll come straight back here. It will give us a chance to work out what we're going to do." I put the emphasis on the word, we.

"We?" She said. "There is no 'we', you made that pretty clear this morning."

"I was in shock this morning." I took another gulp of my tea. Let that thought sink into Ashley's mind. "You've had a chance to get your head around this idea. How long have you known?"

Ashley put her tea cup down and shrugged, "A while." Then she looked down at her hands, avoiding any kind of eye contact with me. "I think I was in denial for a long time. I thought I had a stomach bug, or a cold. But it didn't get any better. Then it started interfering with my work." I could see a large tear forming in her eye and she batted it way like an annoying insect.

"This has ruined my career," she looked up with what could only be described as an intense dislike. "You've ruined my life."

"You opened your legs, darlin'." The words were out of my mouth before I had a chance to take them back.

Ashley stood up, knocking the table, tea ran across the white surface like lava from a volcano.

"It's no use me being here." Ashley strode past me, heading for the door.

I caught her by the arm and spun her round towards me. "You can't keep running away."

Eyes blazing, she tried to pull her arm from my grasp. "Let me go!" she screamed, but I wasn't about to let her go.

Not ever.

"I'm not letting you go. We need to work through this like adults. Now," I said loosening my grip of her arm, but not yet completely prepared to let go, "you haven't answered my question. Can we start again?"

She pulled her arm from my grasp. "What exactly do you have in mind for starting again?"

"Like I said. We spend the next forty-eight hours here. Being together. You can come to the concerts if you want, but I'm not going to force you."

She squinted. "Does anyone else know that I'm pregnant?"

I thought about lying, then thought better of it. If Ashley and I were going to get things sorted out, then lying to her wasn't a great way to start a relationship.

"I told, Murf but he can keep his mouth shut." And he better, or I'd break his freaking knee-caps.

"And if he doesn't?"

"Well, if you go through with this, then everyone's going to know." I couldn't keep the hard tone out of my voice.

"I'm not getting rid of this baby," Ashley said, the hard

line of her mouth telling me that she had made her decision. A ball of concrete settled in my stomach.

"This is not just your decision, the consequences involve both of us." I picked up a cloth from under the bench top and began to wipe up the tea from the table. "And I have the band to think about and my future."

"You don't think I've thought about that," Ashley said her arms crossed and a look of fury painted across her delicate features.

"Look," I said, trying to find a way to diffuse the situation. I was sure that if I could have the next two days with Ashley, we could work something out that would be good for both of us. "Will you agree to stay? No matter what?"

She blinked a couple of times and then turned her back on me, walking over to the large picture window at the end of the room and staring at the view of the city below us.

"I had no idea the city looked like this," she said.

Stood in that large window she looked small and frightened and alone.

Everything inside of me wanted to reach out to her. To protect her. To make her life right.

Somehow, I knew that if things were right with Ashley, then they'd be right with me as well.

There had been so many girls, in hotel rooms, in vans, on the road. She could easily be another invisible girl. Someone I left on the side of the road in another unknown city. But I knew I didn't want that for Ashley. Or for me.

I was tired.

Tired of the superficial nature of touring. Tired of finding another slip of paper on my pillow and not remembering the name of the girl I'd slept with the night before.

It was time for me to take a stand. Do the right thing and take responsibility for my actions.

I covered the ground between us in a moment, slipped my arms around Ashley and allowed her to lean back into me.

The scent of her body and the way she relaxed against mine told me that we were going to get through this.

"Stay with me," I whispered.

"Okay," she replied. Now at least I knew we had a chance. "On one condition."

"What's that?" I asked.

"No posting to your channel for the time that we're here."

She may as well have asked me not to step on stage for the rest of the week.

"You're kidding, right?"

Ashley turned around, slipping her arms round my waist and looking up at me. All I wanted to do was kiss her. She shook her head.

"No. How can we try and work anything out if you're sharing yourself with them?"

I thought I caught a hint of something in her voice.

"They're fans. It's part of the job." How could she ask me to do this? "I have sponsors," I added.

"But you enjoy the adoration."

I couldn't lie. I did.

"So you agree to give them up for the next forty eight hours and I'll put my life on hold and stay here with you."

As far as I could see, I didn't have a choice.

"Okay," I said, "it's a deal. But I'm not leaving you here on your own, you're coming backstage with me when I have to go and do a show."

"If you insist," she replied a hint of a smile beginning to curl the edge of those amazing lips.

"I do," I said giving her a squeeze.

"So, shall we shake on the deal?" Ashley asked, a glint of mischief in her eye.

"I've got a better idea," I said as I gathered her face

between my hands, slanted my mouth over hers and lost myself all over again in the delight that was Ashley.

---

a shley

   As much as I would have liked to have fallen back into bed with Paul, I realised that we weren't going to sort anything out in relation to our future—and the future of our child—if I allowed him to seduce me over and over again.

We ordered a late lunch.

A near banquet was delivered to the room. I decided Paul must have catered for the entire band, not just the two of us.

Lobster tails—which I couldn't eat.

An assortment of seafood that I had to avoid.

A nice looking, mild tropical curry that would probably have given me heartburn. Since I'd fallen pregnant, eating had become a treacherous activity.

I settled on what Paul described as a date scone and a small platter of fruit and tried not to be jealous of the gastro-nomical delights that Paul indulged in.

I sat and watched him devour the food that I couldn't touch with the same enthusiasm that he displayed in so many parts of his life. No wonder his exploits on the internet were so successful. Every activity he engaged in seemed to be an act of pure joy.

He took such pleasure in eating. Now I began to understand why I craved and enjoyed his touch. No wonder his fans loved watching him on stage. I could have sat there all afternoon and simply watched him eat.

As the man devoured lobster tails, cheese and grapes a deep sense of contentment and dare I admit it, love, began to bloom inside of me.

A tiny voice in the back of my head sang warning bells. It tried to remind me that being here wasn't about admiring Paul, it was about trying to work a way forward for me and my baby.

Or should that be our baby?

There went those strange feelings of love, commitment and connection again.

But were they feelings that Paul could or would embrace?

I guessed I would have my answer to those questions in the next forty-eight hours.

Paul sucked the last of the lobster juices from his fingers and then looked at me.

I could feel the heat of a blush as it crept up my face.

"Don't," I said waving my finger at him. "You're not going to seduce me into bed again."

"I must be losing my touch," he said as he pulled the tab off a can of root beer. "Besides," he joked, "we don't have to worry about you getting pregnant."

"That's a low blow," I replied, unable to keep the laughter out of my voice. I realised it wasn't just Paul's body that I found attractive. Hours of watching him on his channel had given me a tiny window of insight into the man—or at least that part of the man he was prepared to share with his fans.

"You said we can start again," I said.

"Yeah," he chugged at the can of root beer, emptying it and then crumpling the can in his hand. A loud belch followed.

"That's disgusting," I snorted, but I couldn't help grinning at him like a stupid schoolgirl. It seemed that Paul took to everything he did with a special kind of enthusiasm.

"Just appreciating the fine food and beverages," he said, flicking a wink at me with that one blue eye.

"Doesn't it annoy you?"

"What?" he asked as he brushed the long locks of hair across his face.

Having your hair in your face all the time.

"Nah." He stopped and thought about things for a minute. "From my experience the world's a heinous and ugly place, the less I have to look at it the better."

"What makes you say that?" It seemed a strange statement for someone to make who lived the kind of cloistered life of privilege that Paul lived. "You get to spend time in places like this," I threw my arms wide taking in again the opulence of the hotel suite. "I've lived in this city all my life and I didn't really believe that places like this existed. You have thousands of fans screaming for you on stage every night. Hundreds of thousands watching your channel. You can have anything you want. How can you say that about life?"

"It's not always been like this," he replied. "I was just a guy who loved playing guitar. I happened to be standing on the right street corner when Julian MacAvoy walked past. He wanted to put together a new band for his brother and the rest, as they say," he shrugged his shoulders, "is history."

"But you had a fantastic tour in Europe."

Paul leaned forward, resting his chin on his hand. "How do you know that? Have you been stalking me online?"

Now I could really feel the heat on my face.

"Come on, spill," he prompted, "you can ask me anything you want, but you gotta be honest with me."

His sincere words, spoken in that accent that still made my insides do a tiny flip and the intense nature of his words, his plea for honesty moved me almost as much as the way he caressed my body moved me.

I didn't look down at my hands. I continued to stare straight into that one blue eye. If we had any chance of making this—whatever this was—work, then I at least knew I had to be honest with Paul.

"Yes," I stammered feeling the rush of embarrassment crawl up my body, "I have been watching your channel."

He stood up from the seat across the table from me. Paul helped me up out of the black bucket chair and then held out his arm, an overwhelming gentlemanly gesture that I wasn't expecting. He waited with infinite patience for me to make up my mind as to whether or not I slip mine through his own. While I stood there deciding what to do he said, "I think we need to make ourselves a little more comfortable. Come and sit with me over here." He pointed with his chin toward a large, grey sofa that had a huge, square chaise attached to the edge of it.

Knowing what a single touch from Paul could do to my body I continued to hesitate to move towards him. "Can you be trusted to keep your hands to yourself?" I half joked. Truth be told, I'd be very happy for Paul's hands to be all over my body—no doubt the reason I was so hesitant to touch him now.

He waved his elbow at me again, encouraging me to slip my arm inside his own. "I guess you're just going to have to take a chance on me."

Was I prepared to take a chance on this man? I was running out of time to decide.

I slipped my arm inside his and an overwhelming sense of comfort flooded through my body. He placed his other hand on my arm and I allowed him to escort me across the expanse of grey and purple designer carpet to the other side of the room. He fussed about arranging the pillows for me and then settled me comfortably down, my back propped against the soft brown cushions that adorned the large grey couch.

Paul pulled another candy-striped pillow from a chair opposite and lay his long frame along the entire length of the chaise. It took all my willpower not to cross the small divide of grey material between us and simply climb on top of him.

He tipped himself over onto his hip and subjected me to his full attention.

"Now," he said, his hair falling away from his other eye, so I could see them both at the same time, "tell me how long you've been stalking me on the internet?"

"Pretty much since Vegas," I muttered. I wanted to squirm in my seat.

A large grin erupted on his face. "You mean even before you found out you were pregnant?"

I nodded, "Yes." I wasn't even embarrassed to admit it any more. I'd been trying to hide the truth from myself for so long, It was exhausting keeping up the charade.

It felt good to admit to Paul that I'd been infatuated with him from the moment that I'd left Vegas.

"Why didn't you email me?"

I shrugged. "I guess I was frightened of how I felt. I figured you gave your email address to everyone. I didn't want to be just another fan." I could hear my heart beating in my ears. The flush of heat that ran through my body made the large room seem suddenly small, cramped and over-whelming.

I took a deep breath and waited for Paul's response.

After a long pause he said, "You know I haven't been able to think of anyone but you since you left Vegas don't you?"

I didn't know whether to believe him. I wanted desperately to believe him. But everything I'd wanted for my life up until I met Paul had suddenly been wiped away by one night in Vegas.

"You can ask Murf tonight," he added, as if trying to drive his point home.

Tonight. I didn't want to think about going backstage with Paul.

"What do the band think about you being here, with me?"

Paul tipped his head to the side. "Who cares what they think. They all know that I've wanted to see you. They probably think we're locked up here fucking. That's what the press will say, anyway."

"The press?"

"Someone will leak that I'm here. They'll be camped downstairs waiting for us. That's why we stay at the venue whenever we can. It's easier."

I hadn't even thought about the press. The hoopla that was Paul's life. How could I have overlooked the freaking press?

"Don't worry about them," Paul said reaching across to stroke the bare skin of my lower leg, "you'll get used to it. I don't even notice them most of the time now. If you stop and give them a photo, they leave you alone. It's if you keep running away that they're a problem."

"I don't want to be in the press," I said. What would my parents think? Stories of me holed up in some hotel room with a rockstar.

Fucking!

Shit. It didn't bear thinking about.

But then telling them I was pregnant didn't bear thinking about either. Maybe I had to stop worrying about what my parents thought of me—or anyone else for that matter. Paul didn't seem to give much thought to what people said about him. I should take his lead.

"It's part of the job," he replied matter-of-factly, "dealing with the press. Once you and I decide what we're doing, then we'll brief Julian and he'll make sure that the appropriate press releases are made." Then he added before I had a chance to digest the last sentence, "But, I'll have to let the channel know first."

I shook my head, trying to get to grips with the information Paul kept firing at me. "You talk about this like it's a given," I said, trying hard not to feel taken advantage of in some insane way. The idea of my life being all over Paul's channel brought back those now familiar feelings of nausea.

"It's a given," he said as if my thoughts on the matter didn't even come into consideration. "My fans have provided me with a life I could never have imagined when I was stuck in London looking for a break. They get to share a part of my life."

He must have seen the fear I tried so hard to hide.

"But they don't get everything," he added. "That's why I said you could ask me anything you wanted to ask me. You've only seen the persona that has been carefully cultivated. I want you to know the real me." I thought I saw a flash of grief cross Paul's face, but I couldn't be sure. Then he brushed his hair aside and stared me straight in the face with an intensity that terrified me. "You do understand that I'm not really that idiot who takes off his shirt and does press ups on stage, don't you? That's a part of the act—the band—what we've built. It's entertainment," he stressed the word as if he were talking to some kind of idiot. Maybe I was an idiot. "It's entertainment that pays for all of this," he spread his arms to indicate the hotel suite, "and it's entertainment that will keep you and pay for our child's education." Paul reached over and took my hand in his. He stroked my fingers with the tips of his own calloused fingers before looking up again into my eyes. "That man on stage, and on my channel, that's not the real me. You've seen more of the real me in the short time we've been together than I've ever allowed anyone else to see."

The real Paul.

Could I believe what he was saying to me?

He seemed so authentic on his channel. The videos I'd

watched. Were they all simply an act? And if they were an act, then who was the real Paul Gray?

I felt the lines form on my forehead as I squeezed my eyes into a tight line as I tried to process the information Paul offered to me. I thought about what I'd watched since Vegas. I think I'd watched everything that Paul had produced. Even though I felt as if I knew the man intimately, what really did I know from the channel?

Was I mixing up my experience with him in Vegas with what I'd learned from the internet?

"Penny for them," Paul said.

"What?"

"Your thoughts. I can see you're wrestling with something. Out with it. I keep telling you that you can ask me anything and I mean it."

Honesty. My head said to me again. As much as I wanted to run from the prospect of sharing my life with this man's fans. It was entirely apparent that if I wanted there to be any kind of future for the two of us and our baby, then I had to deal with his life as it was now.

What were my options, really?

Going home to mom and dad had seemed like a great idea for about fifteen seconds. I couldn't stay in the apartment with Madi, what kind of a life was that for a child? Me with little or no work prospects. Whether I wanted to admit it or not, I needed help. I looked around the palatial surroundings and it was obvious where this help would likely be coming from.

No.

I needed to be smart and besides, if I was honest with myself, the thought of walking away from Paul again.

Well.

I didn't want to go there either.

"Come here," Paul sat up and patted the space next to him.

I did as I was asked and went and sat in the space that his long body had been occupying. I didn't like having to admit that I'd done pretty much nothing but think about Paul since Vegas. All my plans for my life had been pushed sideways. I didn't want to be a simple adjunct to his career. How could I make my way in the world if I was trapped in the hoopla that was his life

Paul slipped his arm around me. A simple gesture of affection. Just being with him made everything so right.

He lifted my chin with his finger and then slipped his lips over mine.

An explosion of feeling erupted from inside of me.

Then everything stopped.

I was aware of nothing except the the touch of his lips on mine. The taste of his tongue as it found its way into my mouth. The callouses on his fingers as they traced a path along my neck.

His fingers twined in my hair.

The scent of him. The bulk of his body as it pressed against my own.

I was powerless in the presence of this man.

When he let me go and rested his forehead against mine, we were both breathing hard. Deep inside, I knew that somehow we had to make this work.

But how?

CHAPTER 13

*P*aul

I'd spent most of the afternoon trying to convince Ashley that she could ask me anything, but she seemed reluctant to delve deeper. We had time, so I wasn't prepared to push.

But I was aware that we didn't have a hell of a lot of time.

I wasn't about to walk away from my responsibilities. That's what my father had done. Left Mum to look after me and my brother and sister.

There was no way that I'd do that to another human being. Even if Ashley and I couldn't make this work, then I'd be there for my child.

The idea of being a father still made me want to hurl my lunch, but I'd never been one to walk away from a challenge or my obligations and responsibilities. I initially wanted to run. Wanted to pretend that Ashley hadn't been pregnant. Stay away from her and bury myself in the music, the women and life on the road.

Then I thought about how I felt after Ashley walked away

from me in Vegas. I couldn't stand the idea of her walking away from me again. No matter what the cost.

I didn't want Ashley dealing with this on her own. It wasn't fair that our actions could destroy her life plans, but that I could continue on with my life as if nothing had happened between us.

Besides, I was over the one night stands. The different girl every night. Never being able to remember anyone's name in the morning. Dancing around a stranger.

Fuck that.

I wanted Ashley and if that meant I had to be a father, then I'd suck that up and get on with it.

Music would always be here for me.

The fans would always be here for me.

But Ashley.

If I didn't act and secure the situation—well there was no guarantee that she would be here for me in the future.

She was so different to the other girls that I'd met on the road.

I wanted her to be a part of my life and I was going to fight to make sure that she stayed with me. One way or another.

Ashley had spent the afternoon dancing around my past and being coy about her own.

But at least now I knew that our night in Vegas was the first time she'd let go of her responsible life and her plan. I'd rolled into her life like a whirlwind and turned everything upside down.

I guess the same could be said for mine.

But maybe, the more I thought about it, maybe my life was ready to be turned around. We might stand on the cusp of something great with Sam, but that didn't necessarily preclude my having a relationship with Ashley, or for that matter a family.

Julian and Mags were managing quite well.

Plenty of other blokes on the road toured with a family. With the money we were making and the money we were likely to make if things kept going well, then I could do whatever the hell I wanted.

The trick. Getting Ashley on board and keeping her on board.

My cell phone went, distracting me from my thoughts.

"The car's outside," I said to Ashley. We were due back-stage for tonight's gig and as per our agreement, Ashley was coming with me.

I watched as she chewed her lip. "You're sure I can't wait here for you?"

"We agreed," I reminded her. Taking in the sensible pair of jeans that she wore. The pale blue hoodie that offset the colour of her blonde hair. She wore her hair in a plait that hung down one side of her face. All I wanted to do was take her to the bedroom, pull out her plait, strip off her clothes and lose myself in the wonder of her body. But I had a show and I wasn't about to let the guys down.

"Will there be press downstairs?" she asked, a tremble in her voice.

I pulled my phone out and pressed Otis' number. "Mate, we got press downstairs? Okay, we're on our way."

"Otis says, no-one's down there."

"We should go then," Ashley said, a hint of a smile brushing her lips. Lips that I'd spent most of the afternoon kissing.

We were taking things slow.

Infuriatingly slow.

The entire relationship seemed to be going backwards.

It was insane. But I wanted to take some time to get to know this woman before the circus of my life took over.

Besides, the anticipation of eventually getting Ashley

back into bed was good for someone like me who was used to immediate gratification.

"You know they're going to find us?" I said as I pressed the button for the lift.

She nodded, "I know. But they haven't yet."

As the lift came to a halt at the ground floor, the doorman met us. "Mr & Mrs Williams," he said, "your vehicle is out the back."

He lead us to the rear of the building and sure enough, Otis stood by the fire exit door, the nondescript car waiting in the back lane.

"You always leave places from the rear of the building?" Ashley asked after I sat down in the backseat beside her. Otis closed the door after me and then settled into the driver's side of the car.

"Only when I don't want to make a scene," I said.

"He's making an effort for you," Otis added as he indicated and pulled out from the kerb. "Normally he thrives on the circus out front."

"It's good for the channel," I added, "entertainment." Ashley nodded. At least now I knew she understood about the entertainment, but the rest of it, I still wasn't sure that she'd come to grips with the circus that was life on the road. "But I'm aware how much you want to stay out of the limelight." *For now.* I thought.

"And you have agreed to stay away from your channel for the next forty-eight hours," she added.

I caught a glimpse of Otis' questioning eyes in the rear view mirror.

"I have," I said, "and I'm a man of my word." Aside from which, as I looked across at the chaste picture of Ashley sitting beside me, I didn't particularly want to share her with anyone—even my dedicated fans.

Maybe it was a good idea to keep a larger part of my life separate from the hoopla that was the life of a rockstar.

"How does Mags cope with all of this?" Ashley asked.

"You should ask her," I said, pressing my hand over Ashley's as the city of Seattle passed by the darkened windows of the car. "She'll be backstage tonight with Julian."

"I don't really know her."

"I thought I saw you talking to her last night."

Ashley's head spun around. "How much do you see from onstage?"

I pecked a kiss on her cheek. "I'm like Otis," the big man's eyes caught mine, reflected in the rear view mirror, "I don't miss a thing."

"Clearly," Ashley said.

The deep baritone voice of Otis filled the small space of the vehicle, "Paul's been scanning the crowd looking for you since Vegas."

"It's not true," I tried to deny it, but only half-heartedly.

"He's not going to let you out of his sight now he's found you again," Otis added.

"I think you should keep your mind on the road," I said trying to shut our good friend up. "I'm surprised that Sam and Julian let you out of their sight."

"Venue's secure," Otis replied. "I'm happy with the security team on the ground. I can't say so much for the hotel or the city."

I felt Ashley stiffen beside me.

"It's not going to take them long to work out you're here," he added.

"I know," I replied squeezing Ashley's hand. "Guess we're going to have you on our tail for the next couple of days."

"Absolutely," Otis replied. "Wouldn't be doing my job otherwise."

"We really need someone with us?" Ashley asked.

"Where did we meet?" I replied. "As I recall, you were wearing a tasty little luminous number with SECURITY emblazoned across the front."

I watched as Ashley's face took on the same blush it took on when I made her come.

"I hadn't really thought about it in the broader sense," Ashley said, "I thought I was just there to make sure no-one got backstage who shouldn't have been there. Do you need someone with you all the time?"

I thought hard about how to answer this question.

Otis saved me, coming to my rescue with his perfect explanation for the uninitiated. "The band needs close personal protection when we're out on tour. We can't be too careful. When they're home, it's a different story. The press leave them alone. And now most of the band are resident in New Zealand, it's not much of an issue at all."

"New Zealand?" Ashley croaked.

Shit!

She looked at me, with what could only be described as terror in her eyes.

"You never said anything about New Zealand. I mean, I know Mags and Julian live there, but you do too?"

I squeezed her hand, trying to reassure her. "We're on the road for nearly two hundred days of the year. Where we live at the moment's pretty irrelevant."

I think her eyes went wider if that could be possible.

"But New Zealand. Where in the hell is that? Somewhere in Holland?"

"No. It's under Australia, down in the South Pacific. Julian moved there first and Sam loves it as well, so we all kind of followed. It's away from the maddening crowds and the people are great. They leave us pretty much alone."

"Really." I didn't know whether she was reassured by my explanation, or whether this was all just too much to be taking in, because for the balance of the car trip we travelled in silence.

When we arrived at the venue, having Otis in the car meant we were waved through by security.

"You still got your backstage pass?" I asked, as I pulled my lanyard with its well worn plastic security tag from my pocket and slung it around my neck.

Ashley squeezed her eyes shut. "Crap. I left it in my pack back at the hotel."

"I'll organise something, don't worry," Otis said as he eyeballed me via the rearview mirror.

I rubbed Ashley's hand. "It's okay, you'll get used to it."

"Will I?" she asked in a tone of voice that sounded a warning shot in my direction, "I'm not quite so sure about that."

She stepped out of the car and slammed the door shut before I had a chance to respond.

The thought crossed my mind that maybe I should have left her back at the hotel.

*a*shley
Despite having been backstage at a Style Strike concert a couple of times earlier, I still felt like a spare part. Everyone rushed around doing some kind of job. The only people who seemed to sit around relaxing were the band members themselves.

I felt completely abandoned by Paul and totally out of my depth in a world that I had absolutely no understanding of whatsoever.

Murf and Griff had said hello when I walked backstage. Sam had acknowledged me with a tip of his head and Dusty was deep in conversation with Mags. The boys called her over to start signing what looked like a mountain of merchandise.

The band members arranged themselves around a large table that could easily have been the centrepiece of someone's dining room. They began to work their way, with a combined lack of enthusiasm, through boxes of disks, posters and assorted branded band paraphernalia.

I sat on an abandoned couch feeling sorry for myself and wondering what the hell I was doing here. I thought about calling Madi and then thought better of it. Besides, she'd be at work by now and she didn't get much time to chat when she was serving fast food.

"Here, put this on," Otis arrived at my side and handed me a black t-shirt that had the band logo on the front and the word, "CREW" in large gold letters across the back. "You won't get thrown out if you wear that and just make sure that you bring your backstage pass tomorrow night, okay?"

I nodded, looking for somewhere private. "Is there somewhere I can change clothes?"

Otis grinned at me, his white teeth seeming somewhat larger than life in the frame of the dark skin of his face. "You're already backstage." He tipped his head toward the multiple clothes racks that adorned one entire side of the room. Each with a band member's name pinned to the top of the rail. "You could strip naked and pin yourself to the wall and these boys wouldn't even notice."

Still, I had my dignity—and I hoped that Paul might at least notice if I paraded backstage naked.

"There's a ladies room out the door at the back and to your right," Otis said. "Please don't go any further until you get that shirt on. I don't want to have to come and rescue you from out front because one of the security guys has been doing his job. Okay?"

I nodded, "Yeah. Gotcha. Oh," I added grateful for Otis' discretion, "thank you."

"You're welcome," he said with a tip of his head. "You'll get used to how things are done."

I wasn't so sure.

I made my way to the ladies room. I found it right where Otis said it would be. I somehow managed to tangle my hair in the zipper of my jacket and was berating myself for my stupidity when Mags walked out of one of the bathroom stalls.

"You need some help?" she asked as she washed her hands and then dried them with one of the tiny, perfectly folded hand towels that lay in a basked on top of the counter.

Tears were welling in my eyes and I swallowed hard. It wasn't like me to lose it simply because I had a problem.

"If I could put my hand on a pair of scissors I'd cut this off right now," I growled, tugging at the end of the hair that had become well and truly tangled in the zipper.

A warm smile crossed Mags face. "Here let me help, Ashley."

"Thank you," I replied, grateful for what seemed like a friendly face in amongst the chaos of back stage. "You remembered my name." She nodded, while I struggled, trying not to pull the hair that seemed terminally trapped.

"You're with Paul," she said her smile turning into a wide grin. "I arranged for Mr & Mrs Williams to be booked into the hotel this afternoon."

I could feel the heat in my cheeks and caught sight of them going scarlet in the mirror opposite me. "What's with that?" I asked, "the Williams thing."

Mags laughed, "Murf's mad on Robbie Williams, it's a bit of a band in joke. Paul wanted to try to keep a low profile."

"I don't get it." Like there were so many things I didn't get about what Paul or the band seemed to find perfectly reasonable.

"Robbie's a British pop mega-star."

I still didn't get it. Mags carefully extracted my hair from the zipper and I sighed with relief.

"So Paul kept a low profile by booking in as Robbie Williams?"

"No, Peter Williams." She waved her hand at me dismissively, "Don't worry. Hang around here long enough and you'll soon get the hang of it all."

"Is it always this mad backstage?"

Mags thought about my question. "Yeah. Like I said, hang around long enough and you'll get a job. People are leaving you alone at the moment. Enjoy it while it lasts."

"Right," I said exchanging my t-shirt for the oversize CREW t-shirt.

"Come find me if you get bored," Mags said, "you won't get much change out of the boys before the show and quite frankly, some of them can be pretty grizzly before they go on."

"Really?"

She nodded. "Don't let them know I told you but nerves and all that."

"Okay." That explained the way Paul had totally abandoned me the moment we stepped foot backstage. I hadn't seen him interacting with the band prior to a show before. I'd only seen him alone, or afterwards, when he was up from the adrenaline rush of being out there in front of his fans. What Mags said started to make some sense. I had no idea who this man was, the one sat at that table signing merchandise with his band mates, shut down inside of himself, waiting to go on stage and be this amazing extrovert.

"They've all got their own little rituals. Do yourself a favour and just stay out of their way until after the show,"

Mags said before she gave me a parting hug and made to leave the ladies room.

"Thanks," I said genuinely grateful for the advice.

By the time I made my way back to the main dressing room where the band were housed, it became apparent that Mags' advice wasn't too far from the truth.

The boys continued to sit studiously around the table, autographing merchandise, but the banter that had been filling the room when I left had ceased. Each had plugged themselves into their own little world. Tiny ear buds, or headsets adorned their heads as they each prepared themselves for their night's work.

I took a seat on the couch across the table within Paul's line of sight. I wanted him to know that I was here for him—whatever that might mean. As I sat there lost in my own thoughts, I began to wonder whether I had any real notion of the man seated at the table just across the room from me.

Almost as if he sensed that I was thinking of him, Paul looked up from the piece of merchandise that he'd finished signing and caught me watching him.

He didn't smile. He simply continued to keep me locked in his gaze.

"Okay?" He mouthed the single word and I nodded a couple of times. The truth of it: I was pathetically grateful that he'd asked, even if it was from across the room. I didn't want him to think that I couldn't handle being here. If there was any chance for us, well then I'd have to get used to being around the band and being backstage. I couldn't think of any other way that we'd be able to support a family, so I had to make this work, if I wanted to keep the baby.

Still, I couldn't imagine what it must be like to live life this way. Every night a different city.

Then there was the bombshell that Paul had dropped in the car on the way here. They lived in New Zealand.

I knew nothing about New Zealand.

Panic washed across me in the same way that nausea had been my recent companion.

What the hell was I contemplating getting myself into now?

CHAPTER 14

*a*shley
     The show was a repeat performance of the one
I'd witnessed the night before and the one I'd watched in
Vegas.

I stood in the wings of the stage and followed Paul,
mesmerised by the way that he moved in the spot of light
that he occupied. I noticed for the first time that he sang
backing vocals in the songs. How had I missed that before?

Now I began to hear the subtle tones of his voice as it
melded with Sam and Griff's in the chorus of each song. I
watched Murf on the drums and began to appreciate the
effort and concentration that went into keeping the band in
time. He counted them into every song and I watched in awe
as the backstage crew worked around each and every band
member. Supporting them. Tuning guitars and generally
being on hand for any kind of unexpected occurrence.

"You're beginning to see the subtle way these guys work
together?" Mags said as she stood beside me.

"Yes," I nodded. Taking note that Julian paced the wings
on the other side of the stage. His facial expressions ranged

from agony to ecstasy in a millisecond, dependant upon whether things were going well, or whether or not something went astray. I knew he would go on stage with his brother for a couple of songs at the end of the second set, but from what I could see, he seemed to hate the experience.

However, it wasn't lost on me that Mags stood on this side of the stage and Julian on the other.

I asked Mags, "How many times have you stood here and watched this?"

"Thousands," Mags said with a smile.

"Don't you ever get bored?"

"Occasionally," she said, "but for the most part every show is different."

"How can it be?" I didn't understand.

"No one crowd reacts the same," she said, "one of the guys might be having an off night. They get a bit sick, or they're hung over, or they're worrying about someone or something." She shrugged.

I wondered whether the last sentence might not be directed at me.

"Julian's been doing this for a long time, hasn't he?"

"He has," she said. "I thought I'd be able to keep him at home in New Zealand, but it was an impossible dream, trying to keep him off the road."

That comment definitely had to be directed at me.

"You like being on the road?"

She shrugged. "Not particularly. But I love my man and being on the road is the price I pay. I tried staying home without him, but I hated it."

"Because of the fans?"

"No. I love Jules' fans. They're responsible for the fantastic life that we're able to lead," Mags said. "If you can't cope with the man that's out there doing what he does to entertain, and the reaction of his fans to him, then you best go and find yourself a nice anonymous bloke who does a nine-to-five job and arrives home every night at the same time."

I swallowed hard.

Mags continued with her friendly advice. "Get out now, while you still can, if you can't cope with what this life entails. Don't think that you can make him choose between you and the band because I can assure you that I've watched so many partners try to do that. He, or she will choose the band over you every time."

Mags sounded so sure of herself stood beside me and looking so relaxed and at ease in her surroundings.

A comfortable silence fell between us. I continued to watch the band and as the guys came to the end of the song, the crowd erupted and another wall of sound rushed across the stage.

Sam and Dusty began the routine that I'd watched them do. I knew that Paul's turn would come soon. He was going to take his shirt off and do those damn push-ups on stage.

He pulled the ear-piece out of his ear and turned to face me and Mags.

Mags leaned in to me and whispered. "He's looking for your approval."

I clapped and a broad grin crossed Paul's face. He turned his back to the crowd and blew me a kiss. A warm glow spread through me. There was something special about being singled out. Knowing that the man up there on the stage, a man so many people wanted, wanted only me.

Whether or not I had the maturity to continue to share him with his fans—that was a question I couldn't answer. Not yet anyway.

"Paul tells me that you live in New Zealand," I said to Mags, "what's it like?"

"It's beautiful and warm and green," she replied, "and the

best part is that in the village where we live, we're treated just the same as anyone else. I love that about New Zealand. The people are great levellers. No-one's impressed by who Jules is or what he does. They just take us as we are."

"It sounds almost like a normal life."

Mags shrugged, "Whatever you like to call normal."

"So how come the whole band lives out there?"

"Jules has set up a label and a studio. We record there, away from everyone. It's a great place for kids as well. Our daughter's grown up there."

"She's here with you now, on tour?" I asked.

"Yeah," Mags nudged me, "Your man's about to get his gear off. I love this bit."

I wasn't sure how to take that. "You do?"

"Paul's so private when we're on the road. I love seeing him behave like this. It's a laugh."

I found myself watching the spectacle of the man I was falling in love with drive the crowd to a frenzy. I saw things that I hadn't seen before. The look on Sam's face as he egged Paul on. I began to see beyond the facade of the entertainers and more into the real men who performed for the baying crowd.

Mags laughed out loud as Paul began to do his press ups and Sam assumed the same position in front of him. Counting directly in his face.

"I haven't seen them do that before," I said.

"They like to mix it up a bit. Probably something they talked about before the show. They need to keep it fresh themselves, or they'll go bonkers."

"Right."

I watched as Paul's muscles flexed under the ink of his skin. A deep longing began to grow inside of me. I may have been carrying this man's child, but standing here now, appreciating his display of strength and beauty, well, I knew I was feeling pretty much the same thing that a lot of the girls in the crowd were feeling.

The difference being, I got to go back to the hotel with him tonight and they didn't.

Maybe that would be enough.

Paul finished his act. As he pulled back on his shirt and strode back to his place on stage, he caught my eye and gave me a big wink.

We may as well have been the only two people on the planet in that moment.

Any thoughts I had of walking away from him vanished.

I was well and truly in too deep—there would be no going back for me.

Not now.

---

*P*aul

Otis accompanied us back at the hotel after the show.

"How come we're coming to the front door?" Ashley asked.

"You see, the mob over there," I pointed in the direction of a gaggle of people who'd appeared at the entranceway of the hotel.

"Oh," she said, "fans?"

"And press," I replied. "If we give them some time, they'll leave us alone."

"How did they find out you were here?"

I shrugged, "Who knows. Hotel staff, or anyone else associated with the venue. We're all public property when we're on the road."

"Mags explained all that," Ashley said with what sounded like a resigned tone to her voice.

"I saw you two talking."

Otis interrupted our conversation. "You ready?"

I looked at Ashley, then pulled her hand to my lips.

"It's okay," she nodded, "I know this is part of it all."

"Let's go," I said to Otis. He climbed out of the vehicle and then attended to the opening of the rear passenger door for me and Ashley. As the door opened and we were exposed to the waiting horde, I made sure that I pulled Ashley to me and kissed her. I heard the shutters going off around us and the car's interior filled with light from the dozens of flash bulbs.

Her eyes were wide with shock, or surprise, I couldn't be sure. I helped her out of the car and held her close to me while we navigated our way through the baying crowd. All the while I was aware that our every move was being documented by explosions of light and people yelling my name.

The cacophony of sound escalated the closer we walked to the hotel's front door.

"Paul. Paul, over here," someone yelled from the depths of the crowd. "Who's the lady. Introduce us," screamed another.

"I thought you said Julian would do a press release," Ashley hissed as she stood by my side, her body ramrod straight, a polite smile painted on her terrified face.

"He will," I reassured her, "but best to get the interest of the press and the fans first." Deciding we'd stood there long enough to generate the required amount of media buzz and to make sure that the press left us alone once we were inside the confines of the hotel, I turned us both around and ushered Ashley inside.

"They won't come in here after us?" she asked.

"A couple of them might check in, but if we stay in the suite, then they can't bother us."

"Of course." She didn't sound convinced, but then who could blame her after that introduction to the press.

We walked past the concierge's desk and he nodded in our direction. "Mr Gray."

"He booked me in this afternoon," Ashley said, "and he knows the booking's under Williams."

"Of course he does," I grinned at her as we waited for the lift. "That's part of the game."

"The game?" she asked.

"Don't worry about it," I touched my finger to Ashley's nose and she wrinkled it in response. "He and his staff will look after us, that's all that matters for now."

The lift doors opened and we both stepped inside.

"I'll see you tomorrow," Otis said from the other side of the doors.

"You're not coming up?" I heard the quaver in Ashley's voice.

"It's okay," Otis reassured her, "I've briefed security. You'll be fine," he turned his attention to me, "unless you're planning to go anywhere tomorrow before the show?"

"Won't be stepping outside the suite until you're in the building," I assured him.

"Goodnight, then," he said as he stepped back and the doors slipped closed.

Ashley and I were alone.

Fuck taking things slow. I'd been watching her from the side of the stage all night.

The show went down well and everyone else would be out somewhere leering it up. I was planning to do some leering it up of my own.

I pushed Ashely against the wall of the lift, trapping her body between me and the glass. My arms pressed against the wall, palms flat on the cool mirror surface.

Her eyes widened again—sporting the same shocked expression that the press caught as she stepped out of the car tonight. My mouth found hers and I lost myself in the sweet taste of her lips.

Ashley's hands snaked up my back and she moaned as I pressed my hips into the cushion of flesh that was her body. The lift came to a halt, jolting me out of my Ashley-induced stupor.

"We're here," she breathed as my lips slid away from hers.

"Let's take this somewhere more comfortable," I said. I realised while I was on stage tonight and while I watched Ashley in the wings that I'd come far too close to giving up the best thing that had ever happened to me.

I wasn't going to be making that kind of mistake any longer.

I had less than forty-eight hours to convince Ashley that we could make this work and I was about to use every weapon at my disposal.

CHAPTER 15

*P*aul

I took Ashley's hand and led her through the plush suite to the sumptuous bedroom. As easy as it was for us to secure entire floors of hotels similar to this one while we were on tour, the band and our management preferred us to stay at the venue in our tour busses.

It wasn't lost on me that the space we were sharing up here was large enough to accommodate most of the people on the tour.

The small pack that Ashley had brought with her for the night lay in the middle of the large bed. Housekeeping had been ordered to stay away from the suite, so the bed hadn't been turned down nor the room tidied. I didn't care. All I wanted to do was to see Ashley spread eagle and naked across the large expanse.

The thought of her intensified the longing that I'd been feeling while I was on stage. I'd taken my shirt off tonight and done my allotted press ups in front of the baying crowd. The roar of them had only done one thing—driven my mind to my overwhelming desire for Ashley.

"Come here," I growled, as I pulled her into my arms. The heat of her flesh, the soft body that I craved, sat tantalisingly close beneath the crew t-shirt that she wore.

"But how do I know that you'll respect me in the morning?" she teased as she leaned her body into mine.

"I'll show you some respect," I replied as my hands found the soft flesh of Ashley's waist. I threw her down on the bed and tugged at her jeans. They came away and I was immediately aware of the musky scent of Ashley's arousal. The only thing that stood between me and the centre of her pleasure, a tiny triangle of yellow cotton edged in white lace.

"Nice," I purred.

Ashley shivered as I stroked the inside of her pale thigh with my rough cheek.

I watched with fascination as her breathing ratcheted up a beat the closer my mouth came to that tiny scrap of cloth.

She had no idea how much I wanted her. How much I wanted to please her and how important it was to me that things went well.

"I need a shower," I said, suddenly aware in the presence of Ashley's warm and tender body, of my own state. "I stink."

She leaned up on her elbows and looked at me.

"I like the way you smell." I watched as she licked her lips. My cock did a dance in my pants in response.

"No," I said. "It's not fair to bring the stench of the show to bed with you."

Two hours on stage was always a workout. No matter what, I always needed a shower after a show. It was the full stop that brought me back to the reality of my life. I washed away the persona that I'd become on stage.

Standing under the heat of the water gave me a chance to come back to ground.

As much as I wanted Ashley, I also wanted Ashley to know me—the real me—not the carefully crafted persona that I became when I walked on stage with the rest of the band.

"Come on," I pulled Ashley up off the bed. I'd nearly let my overwhelming desire to fuck her get in the way of my own personal standards. Besides, the thought of spending some time worshiping her body under the shower appealed. Not something I'd ever have been able to do in the tiny postage-stamp sized bathroom in the van I shared with the boys.

The bathroom that adjoined the bedroom suite was easily triple the size of the living area that the three of us enjoyed. In keeping with the artsy nature of the boutique hotel, the entire room had been done out in gold and red.

"I keep forgetting how gold it is in here," Ashley sighed as we stepped onto the warmed tiled floor.

Golden mirrors with elaborate frames that wouldn't have been out of place in an antique show room filled one entire wall. As I removed the balance of Ashley's clothing, her ample curves were reflected back to me from various angles. It was like standing in some strange, pornographic carnival ride. It only fuelled my desire, seeing her body in so many different ways.

Thick red tassel rugs were strewn across the tiles in front of the large, sunken bath. Two huge golden lions stood guard at either end of the triangular tub, their mouths ready to spurt water into the tub at the turn of a tap.

The toilet and the bidet which sat adjacent to the bath sported matching golden fittings. I shrugged out of my own damp, sweaty clothes and turned my attention to the enormous shower which stood on the other side of the room.

A bank of golden controls sat beside a wall of glass. I opened the door and turned my mind to working out how to make the seven shower heads pump water into the space.

The overhead rectangular rain shower sputtered into life.

On its own it would have been enough to make sure that Ashley and I were covered in water, but I wanted to play. I watched as the water ran across the pebbled concrete floor to the drain hidden in river stones at the end of the glass enclosure. I stepped under the tepid shower—the temperature made me catch my breath.

Ashley laughed. "Cold?"

"You'll warm me up," I said as I pulled her in after me.

Her squeal of delight as the water hit her body did more to me than the twenty thousand fans who'd been calling my name tonight.

Droplets of water ran down her body and I had the urge to follow them with my tongue. Instead, I pressed buttons and turned dials until I had all seven of the shower heads blasting warm water across the entire space. We were being assaulted from all sides.

"Oh my god," Ashley purred as she turned her body around in tiny circles, allowing the water to caress her.

I ripped the paper from a large cake of soap and began to chase the water across Ashley's skin.

The sweet scent of rose filled the warm damp air around us. As my hands and the suds slipped across Ashley's body she began to relax.

"You like?" I asked.

She nodded, "Hmm, very much. I could get used to this if you're not careful."

Those were the kind of words I wanted to hear.

She took the soap from my hand. "Let me do you."

I watched Ashley's tiny hands as they struggled with the large cake of soap. Water and bubbles cascaded from my own body down her breasts and stomach as she continued to wash me with delicate strokes.

My cock stood between us, hard as iron, the promise of pleasures to come.

When her hand slipped around and gripped the girth of me, I sucked in a breath.

"Careful," I said, "I'm dangerous when I'm aroused."

Ashley looked up at me, droplets of water running down her face. "I laugh in the face of danger," she said and then she did just that.

When her hands cupped my balls and she squeezed I couldn't stand it any longer.

My mouth fell upon hers and I pulled her body to me.

"I need to get out of here," I growled, as I hit the master switch and cut the water.

I'd have been happy to lick Ashley dry, but instead I wrapped her in a thick, red towel and quickly dried myself. Her long blonde hair coiled itself into damp dreadlocks down her back. I gathered it in another towel and massaged the vast amount of liquid out of it before leading my beautiful lady back to the bedroom.

I pulled back the cover on the bed and lay her down on the sheets. As much as I wanted to fuck her senseless, I wanted to make this moment last.

As I traced the curve of her stomach with my lips, I could smell the lingering scent of rose on her warm skin. I ran my hands up past the angle of her hips to the rise of her breasts. Large, dark nipples begged for my mouth and Ashley gasped as I sucked a nipple into my mouth.

Her body arched under me and my fingers found their way to the wetness between her legs.

As I slipped a finger inside of her she moaned. "I need you."

"I need you too, my sweet," I said as my lips crashed down on hers.

Ashley's tongue found its way into my mouth as my rock hard cock found its way home inside of her.

She moaned and thrust her hips up against me.

Our bodies writhed and pounded into each other on the crisp, cool sheets.

Ashley was my everything. I could easily give it all up.

The music.

The money.

The fame.

All to be here inside of her now like this.

I was home and it was where I wanted to stay.

Forever.

---

*A*shley

We spent the morning making slow and languid love, between eating morsels of food that Paul ordered from room service.

I wanted to believe that it could be like this forever. Just the two of us. No-one making demands. Nobody in the way of us getting to know each other.

Making plans for a future together.

I had moments of feeling as if I were participating in some kind of alternate universe. Surely, things couldn't work themselves out this well. Something had to go wrong.

Didn't it?

Paul sat propped up on the large bed, surrounded by crisp, white pillows. The ink on his skin a stark contrast to his pale surrounds.

"Does it hurt?" I asked as I traced the crimson petals of the large rose tattooed across his beating heart. Each time his heart beat a petal fluttered under my fingertips.

Paul shrugged, "Sometimes. It depends where it is."

"Did this one hurt?" I stroked my fingers across the edge of each petal, the colour going from crimson to almost black.

"A bit," he replied, "but I was drunk most of the time."

"Why do you do it if it hurts?" I couldn't understand the fascination anyone had with covering their body in ink. Especially if it involved pain.

"I like the way it looks," he replied, "and it helps me mark the passing of important occasions in my life."

"Why did you have this put here," I asked, tracing the rose over his heart.

"My mum loved red roses," he said. "So when she died, I had this tattooed over my heart."

He'd never talked about his parents.

"I'm sorry you lost your mom," I said, grateful that my own parents were still here and both living in this city. I had no idea what they were going to make of Paul, or the news that I was carrying his baby. "What about your dad?"

"I never knew him," Paul said a bitter edge to his voice. "He didn't want kids and he left my mum to bring us up by herself."

A churn of nausea coiled inside of me.

"You don't have any contact with him at all?"

Paul shook his head, "Nah."

"That must be hard."

"It's what it is," he replied in a matter-of-fact tone. "I've never known him so I figure he's the one missing out. From what mum said he's a fucked up old drunk anyway. I hope he dies alone in a ditch somewhere. Who gives a fuck?"

I wondered whether or not Paul gave a fuck.

"He's never come looking for you?"

"He contacted management when I was touring Europe. When they worked out he was only looking for money they told him to get lost. He threatened to go to the papers, so Julian took care of it. Told them all that they wouldn't get a decent story from me or the band ever again if they printed anything he had to say. That put an end to it."

I stroked Paul's shoulder, his body felt like stone under

my touch. Every muscle tense. Too tense. Talking about his father hurt him. No wonder he'd been so stressed about my pregnancy news. He hadn't exactly had the perfect family life. Was the child that I carried destined for the same kind of dysfunctional upbringing?

I shuddered at the thought.

"Anyway," he said, turning on his side and facing me, his body taking on a languid feel, as if he'd banished the past from his mind. "I don't want to talk about me. What about your parents? What do they think about you being pregnant?"

The heat of a blush began to crawl its way up my body.

"Fuck!" Paul's eyes went wide, "You haven't told them."

I averted my gaze, trying to look at anything. Concentrating on the flashes of purple that trailed through the designer carpet, the chrome of the perfectly proportioned chair that sat in the corner of the bedroom suite. Anything but Paul.

"You need to tell them," he said his voice softening. He tipped my chin up so that my eyes had to meet with his.

"We can tell them together."

The sound of that appealed to me.

"I didn't want to tell anyone until I told you."

"And I appreciate that," he said. "I need to apologise for the way I behaved, when you first told me."

"It's understandable," I said. It made so much more sense to me now that I knew Paul had never known his own father.

"You know that I'm not going to run out on you, don't you?"

I still couldn't be sure, but I nodded, trying to reassure who? Me or Paul?

"I mean it." Paul said as if he could read my mind. "I'm not going to behave like my father. I want this to work for us."

"I know."

The fact that I still couldn't see how it was ever going to work for the two of us with him being on the road and me trying to bring up a child somewhere in the world didn't seem to matter. It appeared that Paul had made up his mind and from what I'd seen of the man, on and off the stage, determination wasn't something lacking from his nature.

Still, the idea of taking him home to meet with my parents turned my blood to cool ice in my veins.

How the hell was I going to introduce a rockstar to my straight-laced parents and tell them that they were going to be grandparents in the same afternoon?

Running away and hiding out on the road with Paul and the band had a sudden appeal that I'd not appreciated before.

CHAPTER 16

*P*aul
As much as I'd liked to have stayed holed up with Ashley forever in the hotel, languidly making love and feeding her morsels of food. Unfortunately, reality called. Its name was Otis and he'd arrived to collect us again for the second-to-last night in this city.

I knew if nothing else that I had one more night here with Ashley before the band had to be back on the road to complete the tour.

I had one more night to convince her that we could have some semblance of a life together—whether it be on the road or whether it be somewhere else in the world.

Realistically, while Sam's star was on the rise, we needed to be spending more than two hundred days a year on the road. With Julian negotiating an extension of the tour who knew how long we could be living in vans anywhere in the world. That meant that by my calculation, if we had a break in the tour and then headed out again, I'd still be on the road when the baby was due to be born.

What kind of life was that for Ashley?

How the hell could we sensibly keep a family and a relationship together while I was touring all over the world?

The alternative—fuck! There wasn't an alternative. I didn't spend all those months playing in the Tubes in London to give it all away because Ashley was going to have a baby.

We had to find a way to make this work.

As much as I knew I loved Ashley, the music remained my master. If I didn't do something with my music, I may as well not be above ground breathing. I couldn't even rely on my channel bringing in enough to keep us. It had become abundantly clear that the tour and the band was the reason that my popularity had exploded.

Take away the band and the tours and I was left with nothing.

Well, not exactly nothing. I had Ashley and the baby, but there would be nothing left of me.

I couldn't go home and get a nine-to-five job. Ashley would come home one day and find me hanging from the nearest light fitting.

No.

There had to be a way to make this work.

If Julian and Mags could do it, then so could me and Ashley. All I needed to do, was get on side with Julian and find out what was the secret to his success. Mags and their baby girl seemed happy. At least what I'd seen of them both on tour. Granted they hadn't been here the entire time, but the time that they had been on the road, it looked as if everything went well for their little family.

I wracked my brain, trying to think of other examples of rockers who'd taken their families on the road with them.

I drew a blank.

Fuck!

I dug my phone out and started googling. There must be

someone in the midst of internet-land who had a stellar record of managing on the road with a family, besides Julian and Mags.

What was wrong with Julian and Mags? I pondered that thought for a moment.

"Are you sure I can't stay at the hotel tonight?" Ashley eyed me with what looked like reluctance to head out of the hotel. This didn't bode well for a future on the road together.

"I thought you enjoyed being backstage with me," I said, hoping to jolly her out of whatever kind of reluctance had taken hold.

"Being backstage is okay," she said, "but it's the getting through the crowd out the front of the hotel that I don't like."

"You'll get used to it." Would she, I wondered? I knew I couldn't let Ashley stay at the hotel tonight. "The press will be expecting you to come with me. We can't let the fans down, now can we?"

Ashley took a deep breath and gave me a weak smile. "Guess not."

"Look," I scrubbed my face with my hand, "I know the press are a pain in the arse."

She laughed.

"What are you laughing at?"

"The way you say ass."

"What about the way I say arse?"

"It's cute."

Did I like being described as cute?

Ashley surprised me by getting out of bed and showing some kind of enthusiasm for getting ready for the show. "What are your fans demanding that you do on stage tonight?" And she surprised me by completely changing the subject.

I shrugged, "I don't know."

"What do you mean?"

"I haven't looked at my channel."

"Why not?" She was pulling on a pair of jeans that I wanted to peel off her again.

"I promised you that I wouldn't look, so I have no idea what they want me to do. Probably the usual."

Ashley clipped an apricot bra in place, covering her appealing nipples—another piece I had the urge to rip right off her—then stopped getting dressed. She turned to face me and said, "You mean you haven't looked at your channel since we've been here?"

"No. I keep my promises."

A look of confusion crossed her face and then it was as if she realised what I'd said. "You'd do that for me? Not take a look at your channel?"

I nodded. "I'm a man of my word."

"But your fans?"

"One of the boys will tell me what they want."

Ashley pulled a tiny pink t-shirt out of her bag and shuffled her ample curves into the tight material. I wanted to touch her. I wanted to be in bed with her again, enjoying every inch of her appealing body.

Fuck work.

When did music become work?

I loved music. I loved my fans.

But I think I realised in that moment I loved Ashley more.

———

*A*shley
    "Paul, Ashley, over here!" One of the photographers who had remained at the front of the hotel called out the second we stepped foot outside the safety of the hotel foyer.

"How do they know my name?" I hissed at Paul.

154

"There's not much that they won't know by the end of the tour," he replied.

We stopped in front of the bank of photographers and I remembered to smile. I hoped that my parents didn't read any of the gossip sites and I doubted that the mystery woman that Paul Gray had on his arm would make the network news.

But it was becoming apparent that I had to tell my parents what was going on—before they found out from the press. And lord only knew what else the press knew about me already.

By the time Otis had us stowed in the car and we were on our way back to the concert venue, I'd pulled out my phone. With trembling fingers, I pressed the number for my parents' home.

"Who you calling?" Paul asked.

"My parents," I replied as I waited for the phone to connect.

"What are you going to tell them?"

I put my hand on his leg. His thigh felt like steel through the thick, blue denim. "Just that I'm seeing you. Nothing else." The muscle of his leg physically relaxed under my touch.

"Mom," I gave Paul a reassuring smile as I heard the familiar greeting of my mother.

"Yes, I know." I said, agreeing that it had been a while since I'd called. I felt guilty about that, but there was so much happening in my life that I'd wanted to hide from my parents. I didn't want them worrying about me—I was doing enough worrying for everyone.

"Look," I needed to cut to the reason for my call, "I'm seeing someone."

Her squeal of delight told me far more than I wanted to know. I'd been too busy with my studies to have anything to do with a man for such a long time and now, as much as my mom thought that I wasn't a whole person without a man on my arm—I couldn't be sure how pleased she would remain when she found out exactly who I had on my arm.

"He's in a band," Paul started to play up next to me. Sticking out his tongue, trying to lick me behind my ear. I couldn't wriggle out of his way. I held my hand up trying to block his advances, but he was clearly enjoying the game. Making me laugh—despite the difficulty of talking to my mother.

I gave him a hard stare.

He ignored me and tried to slip his hand between my legs.

I trapped it in my thighs and then pinched his nipple.

He yelped.

I held my finger to my lips, telling him to be quiet.

Paul lifted his hands up in surrender and pulled himself to the far side of the car, leaving me to concentrate on my mother's inquisition

"They're playing here in Seattle and I'm staying with him. I wanted you to know because there were some press out the front of the hotel."

Mom asked me half a dozen questions in quick succession—it was enough to make my head spin.

"Look," I said, "I'm not sure how his schedule is tomorrow, but why don't I see if we can pop down and say hello."

Paul's eyes went wide.

"Okay then," I said keeping my eyes on Paul the whole time. "I'll check his schedule and I'll get in touch with you tomorrow. Love you too. Bye."

I slipped my phone back in my jacket and looked at Paul.

"They want to meet you. How about tomorrow?"

Paul leaned forward, attracting Otis' attention. "You free to ferry us to the suburbs tomorrow?"

"Let me know where and I'll check it out," Otis said.

"It's my parents house," I replied, since when could my parents be considered a security risk?

"Give me the details," Otis said, "and I'll check it out."

Huge eyes stared back at me from the rear view mirror. Otis wasn't someone I wanted to piss off.

Paul pulled his backstage pass from his pocket and hung it around his neck. I did the same, grateful tonight that he'd reminded me to put the small piece of plastic in my bag.

"Have you worked out what your fans want you to do?" I asked.

"I told you," Paul said, giving me a squeeze, "I haven't looked at my channel."

"Don't be silly," I said pulling my phone back out of my jacket. I dialled up Paul's channel and then froze.

"What's the matter?" I could hear the edge of concern in his voice.

I opened my mouth, but nothing came out.

He pulled the phone from my hand.

"What the fuck?"

"You promised me you'd never post that," I said as I looked at the video of me and Paul in bed in the van.

"I didn't post it," Paul said in a strangled tone.

"Well how the hell did it get on your channel?" I still couldn't believe what I was looking at. Under the video sat notes explaining that Paul had met me in Vegas and we were here in Seattle together.

His fans wanted me on stage tonight.

That wasn't going to fucking happen.

CHAPTER 17

*P*aul

Ashley had stormed ahead and locked herself in the ladies as soon as we arrived backstage.

No amount of banging on the door was getting her attention.

"Leave her alone, man," Griff said.

"You'll smash the door down if you keep that up," Murf added.

"What's gotten up your arse?" Griff had me by the arm and pulled me back towards where Murf stood a couple of feet from the bathroom door.

"This!" I yelled, flashing a shot of Ashley and me in a clinch to the two of them. The shots of her naked in my bed followed soon after. These were for my viewing pleasure only—not for the fans or the channel. It didn't take a genius to work out what was going on. The short video had already gone viral.

"Fuck," Murf said, "I'm so sorry mate.

We both looked at Griff.

I didn't need to put two and two together.

"Yeah, great publicity don't you think?" he sounded pleased with himself.

"No, I don't fucking think," I screamed as I lunged for him. "Are you responsible for this?" I yelled only inches from his face.

"Fuck you!" He spat. "You can thank me later, when you've thought about it." He really thought that he'd done something good.

"Jesus!" I walked away. If I stood in front of him any longer, I was likely to punch him and I didn't need to get in a fight this close to going on stage.

"Problem lads?" Julian arrived at our side, concern painted on his face. Mags stood beside him and they passed a knowing glance. They communicated without even saying a single word. I wondered what it must be like to have that kind of intimate relationship. They way things were going with Ashley, I couldn't see us ever having the kind of intimacy that Mags and Julian shared. Especially when a 'supposed' friend decided that splashing shots of her all over the internet would help matters.

"Are you two behind this?" I asked my hands clenching and unclenching at my side. If I didn't do something with them I swear that I'd hit Griff.

"No," Mags answered. "Is Ashley in there?"

"Yeah, and she won't come out."

"I'll go talk to her," Mags said giving Julian a *get-him-out-of-here* look.

"I'm not going anywhere with him," I sulked pointing my chin in the direction of an uncomfortable looking Griff.

"Fuck off, Ryan," Julian said with a tilt of the head.

"I was only trying to help," Griff complained as he walked away.

"Go sort him out," Julian said to Murf.

"You cool, man?" Murf said to me.

I nodded, "Yeah. Go make sure that fucking keyboard player doesn't get himself smashed before we go out there tonight."

"I've got this," Julian said to Murf, like I was some kind of kid that needed looking after. The implication stung. I hadn't needed looking after ever.

"Come on," Julian pointed in the direction of the band's backstage lounge. I walked beside him, a maelstrom of emotions churning through me. "You need to pull yourself together," he said. "You've got a job to do on stage and you can't let this kind of shit get in the way." He shook is head, "I knew that fucking channel of yours was going to get us in the shit one day."

"There's nothing wrong with the channel," I said as I threw myself down onto one of the couches in the lounge area that had been provided for us backstage. "It's the idiots that think they know what they're doing that are the issue. I'll kill that fucker if he gets anywhere near me."

"Shut the fuck up." The tone of Julian's voice startled me.

"What?"

"You heard me." He sat down opposite me. "I don't know what's going on between you and that girl."

"Her name's, Ashley."

His face softened, "You and Ashley." He made a point of extending the last vowel sound and now I wanted to punch him as well. "But I've been on the road long enough to know that if you really want to make it, you can't let anything get between you and Ryan or the band is fucked."

I didn't like hearing what he was saying. Griff might well have terminally pissed me off, but I also knew that I didn't want to be in a band where I hated someone I had to live and work with for three quarters of the year.

The truth hurt more than the agony I was in over Ashley.

"Why did he have to do that?" I whined. Even I thought I sounded pathetic.

Julian pulled his phone out of his pocket. "Have you looked at the hits you've had lately?" He took one look at my face. "I thought not. Too busy fucking yourself senseless up in that grand hotel suite."

I wasn't even going to acknowledge that statement.

"Take a look," Julian held his phone out towards me. With my promise to Ashley still fresh in my mind and with some reluctance and a raging case of resentment, I took the offered phone from his hand.

"Fuck…" I couldn't believe what I was seeing. The footage of me and Ashley together had almost trebled the recent interaction I'd been having.

"They're demanding that she come on stage with me tonight," I said. "She'll never agree to it."

"You stay away from her and let Mags deal with it," Julian said as he took his phone back from me. "You need to get your head in the game for the show."

I knew Julian was right. I couldn't imagine that Ashley would ever agree to coming on stage with me.

"Why do they want her on stage, anyway?"

"She's a child of the city—one of their own. She's been holed up for two days in a hotel room with you," Julian replied. "You're supposed to be so *market savvy*," he twitched his fingers in the air as he said the last two words, "I can't believe you're even asking me that question."

My head dropped into my hands and I moaned. "How the fuck did this happen?"

Julian stood up and slapped me on the back. "It's a consequence of being on the road, pal, get used to it." He started to walk away, but then stopped and turned back to face me. "Go and make it up with Ryan you two have got a show to put on tonight."

As much as I still wanted to give Griff a great big thumping, I knew Julian was right. No matter what happened with Ashley, I still had to be on the road with the boys for more than two hundred days a year.

I let out a deep sigh and stood up. I knew exactly where to find Griff.

Ashley

I stood over the cold ceramic basin in the ladies room and didn't know whether to puke in it, or run some water in it to wash the tears from my face. I didn't want to let Paul see me cry.

It had become apparent to me in the last few moments in the car that there was no way we were going to be able to make this work. I simply wasn't cut out to cope with the way Paul's life played out in front of the nation.

How could I take someone like him home to my parents?

How could we even begin to pretend that we could have any kind of life together with him being out on the road for most of the year?

I'd spent almost two days holed up with him in a hotel room. It was a complete fantasy. I don't know what I was thinking even coming to see him, or letting him know that I was pregnant.

I'd been stupid.

I'd been careless and now I was going to have to pay the price for that one night of carelessness for the rest of my life.

The tears continued to fall down my face and I let them splash onto the hard surface of the basin.

His life was with the band—up on stage—living every moment out in the spotlight for everyone to consume. I didn't want a life like that. I wanted a stable career, a sensible home life and more than anything not to have my life laid out bare for strangers to pick over like a carcass decomposing in the desert.

I shuddered.

How did these people live like this?

The door to the ladies room flew open and I looked up, rubbed the tears out of my eyes and readied myself to tell Paul to go away.

"Oh, it's you," I said unable to hide the relief in my voice as Mags walked in.

All the fight left my body and I slumped in front of her. My shoulders sagged and all I wanted to do was sit down. The purple chaise that sat across the other side of the well appointed ladies restroom suddenly took on an appeal that surprised me.

"How you doing?" Mags asked, a hint of concern in her British accent.

"You really want to know?"

She shook her head in affirmation, "Yes, I do want to know. I remember how it feels to be standing about where you're standing now."

"Really?" I wasn't sure whether to believe her or not, "you've spent a fair amount of time hiding in the ladies room as well?"

"You could say that," Mags' voice held the hint of laughter, "Hiding in Public we call it."

The words of the song that Sam and Julian sang flooded into my mind. "So that's what the song's about."

Mags shrugged. "Who knows with songwriters? It could be about the cat we have back home," she screwed up her face. I knew what she was trying to do. Attempting to make me feel at ease and all of a sudden, I was grateful for a woman to talk to.

"How did you know I was in here?" I wiped the last of the

tears from my face with the sleeve of my sweatshirt. At least having her here had shut down my overwhelming urge to sit in a pit of sorrow.

Now she did laugh. "I followed the bellowing and found Paul outside the door." She shrugged. "Easy-peasy."

I eyed the chaise again and Mags followed my gaze.

"Why don't you go and sit down for a while," she said, "gather your thoughts and I'll go and find us something to drink and we can talk about what's been going on."

"I'd rather go back to the hotel," I said, "or maybe I should just go back to my apartment."

"You're not going anywhere," Mags said in a stern tone that took me by surprise and that I knew meant business. "You and I need to talk some things through." I must have looked as uncomfortable as I felt because Mags' voice softened. "Look, if you still feel that way after we've had a chat, then I'll arrange myself for someone to see you safely back to your apartment, how does that sound?"

It sounded like a deal. "Okay," I said, "I'll stay and hear you out."

"Good," Mags said as she put her hand on the door handle. Before she opened the door, she turned back to me, "While I'm gone, you might like to think about what you running away would do to Paul. He's due on stage shortly and he has a job to do. What would his being in the wrong headspace because of you do to the rest of the band, do you think?"

She left and I sat staring at the door—not wanting to think.

Then I got angry.

The cool space I sat in seemed suddenly warm and oppressive.

How dare she fucking suggest that I had anything to do with what might happen to a band before they went on stage.

The nerve of the woman.

Then I started to think it through.

And the more I thought about it, the more I realised that running out on a guy just before he was due to go on stage wasn't the smartest thing to be doing about now.

I dropped my head in my hands.

"Why?" I said to no-one in particular.

Why had the universe done this to me?

Hadn't I been an A plus student? Hadn't I done everything that I was supposed to have done all the way through school and then college? Why the hell had a supposed one night stand turned into this kind of a nightmare?

I couldn't even bring myself to blame Madi any more for the mess I found myself in.

If I was honest, I'd fallen for Paul. A part of me wanted this bizarre excuse for a relationship to work. A part of me wanted to have his baby and for everything to work out for us—but right this minute, I couldn't fathom how that was ever going to happen.

How did I find myself sitting on a purple chaise, backstage with a man whose fans wanted me out there on stage with him tonight?

This was not part of the grand plan I had for my life.

My body still ached every time I thought about Paul's hands caressing me. The way they made me feel this morning.

Damn it. I could still smell him on my skin.

He completed me in a way that no-one had ever completed me before.

The thought that those same hands, with the little calluses on his fingertips that made me squirm, might caress anyone else in the future did things to me that I couldn't begin to articulate.

The door opened and Mags walked back into the room with two bottles of sparkling water.

"I figured I couldn't go too wrong with this?" she said as she handed me one of the small blue bottles and then handed me a green plastic cup as well. "You might want something stronger, but I never like to encourage anyone to drink before the show."

"Thanks," I said as I took the bottle from her hand and made haste to unscrew the white cap. All the while I wondered if she knew that I was pregnant and she might be waiting for me to confide in her.

If she knew, it was because Paul had told her and I was ready to notch that up again as a mark against him. I needed ammunition to hate him and at the moment there was very little I could pin on him except the social media breach.

It suddenly dawned on me that the social media breach may not have been Paul's fault.

Had Mags done this?

How did I ask her something like that?

We sat in strained silence. Mags didn't say a word, simply drank her drink and waited. For what? Me to open up and tell her what was going on? *Maybe that's not a bad idea.* A sensible voice in my head said. If anyone knew how hard it was to live with someone on the road, it would have to be Mags.

When I couldn't stand the silence any longer I asked, "How do you do it?"

"Do what?"

"Live your life out in the spotlight with Julian and Sam and the band?"

"I only have to share a little of my life when they're on the road. It's not onerous." She put her bottle down on the floor. It struck me as strange that no-one had walked into the bathroom the whole time we had been there.

"Does everyone know we're in here?"

Mags threw me a look of what? Pity. "We're on tour. Everyone knows what's going on with everyone else. That's how it is on tour. Why do you think Paul booked you both into a hotel?"

"I hadn't thought it through."

"Because he wanted the two of you to have some privacy."

"Oh." Now I felt stupid and selfish and ungrateful.

"Look," Mags said, "I know you're upset about the stunt that Griff's pulled-"

I cut her off, "Upset doesn't even begin to describe how I'm feeling right now."

"Okay, I get it," Mags said as she pushed her backstage pass to one side to pick at some imaginary speck of something on her pale blue jeans. "But, like I've said before, if you're going to tie your wagon to the likes of Paul then you're going to have to cut him some slack with the fans."

"But why does he have to play his life out on stage for the world to see?" I could hear the desperate whine in my own voice.

"I think I should tell you a story," Mags said, as she picked the bottle of water up off the floor and made a point of taking a large drink, before she screwed the top back on and put it down again.

The woman had my rapt attention and I wasn't even sure why.

CHAPTER 18

*P*aul

I trudged back to the van, my hands buried deep in my pockets. I didn't particularly want to be having this conversation with the lads, but I knew that Julian was right.

Sam stepped out of his and Dusty's trailer and met me with a broad smile. He looked nothing like the rock god that would grace the stage tonight. He had on one of Julian's old tour t-shirts with 'crew' emblazoned across his back and a pair of jeans that were cut and pinned in a way that looked as if they'd been worn every night since we'd been on the road.

"Great job getting the locals revved up for tonight's performance," he said as he held his hand up for a fist bump.

I obliged, allowing him to pull me into a tight hug and feeling less than thrilled about the reason for the congratulations. "You need to thank Ryan, it was his doing." I bit out the words, the bile forming in the back of my throat. How the hell Ashley was going to get past this, I didn't know. It was one of the things that she'd been so adamant about right from the first moment that I'd met her. That was one of the things that had attracted me to her—she wasn't looking for any kind of limelight. Now I'd brought this down on her. Well, Griff had brought it down on her, the bastard.

"Your channel and your platform," Sam said have been the making of this tour. "You've gotten us exposure here that we couldn't have gotten any other way. I'm grateful, man."

That said a lot, coming from Sam.

I needed to remind myself that without Sam and Julian I'd still be busking in the London Underground with Murf. Griff may have pissed me off, but we were all still in this together.

"Julian backstage?" Sam asked after his older brother.

"Yeah," I nodded, "he was in the band lounge when I left."

"Later," Sam said, and went to walk away. Then he stopped. His face creasing with concern. "You and Ashley okay?"

I shrugged, "Waiting to hear from Mags on that one."

"Mags will sort it," Sam said, "she always does."

He sounded like a man whose issues had been untangled one too many times by his sister-in-law. "If you say so," I said not having the same conviction as Sam.

"She will," he said the throwaway comment lingering in the carpark as he walked away.

I pulled open the door of our van. The place that I'd been calling home for more nights than I could remember. The familiar stench of three men living together in a confined space was somehow comforting. I found Murf and Griff sitting in the small lounge area, both plugged into their own electronic worlds.

Murf acknowledged my entrance with a tilt of his chin, but Griff ignored me.

It was going to be like that.

I hated eating humble pie—but for the sake of the band I was prepared to meet Griff half way.

"Griff!" I yelled.

He looked up at me with those familiar eyes of his that had been nothing but pools of pain the entire time we'd been on the road. No wonder he wanted to anaesthetise himself every night after the show. That girlfriend had really fucked him over. I'd never understood his pain, now I had an inkling of what he might have been going through.

"What?" Hostility rolled off the single word. He pulled his headphones off his head and made a point of staring at me, waiting for me to open the conversation.

Where to start. I scrubbed my hand through my hair. "Julian doesn't want us to fight."

"Since when have you ever given a fuck about what Julian wants," Griff made to put his headphones back on again.

"Hear me out." I was useless at this. Griff, to give him his due, hesitated long enough for me to take a deep breath and start again. "What you did was wrong."

"Fuck off!" Griff yelled. "You've built a channel on your out-of-control escapades with groupies, what's the difference this time?"

I lunged for him.

Murf had me in a death-grip before I even got half-way across the room. "What would Robbie do?" He asked as he pushed me down on the couch.

"Fuck, Robbie!" Griff and I said in unison.

Then we stopped, looked at each other and collapsed in a fit of laughter.

"I'm sorry, man," Griff said, "I didn't know she meant that much to you."

"Well, she does," I said wiping the tears out of my eyes.

"You want me to go talk to her?"

"Nah," I replied, "Sam tells me that Mags will fix it. Mags can fix anything."

"I think she probably can," Murf agreed. "If she's been on

the road with the MacAvoy brothers forever she's got to be able to do something right."

"You think Ashley will come on stage tonight?" Griff asked, "it's what your fans want."

I shrugged, "No idea. Don't even know if she'll be here after the show. The state she's in." The thought made my stomach turn over. I didn't want Ashley to leave, but I'd worked out I had little control over the woman.

"Sorry mate," Griff said, "I thought I was doing the right thing."

No doubt he did. If anyone knew how it felt to be rejected by a woman, it was Griff. I almost felt sorry for him.

"Ashley wouldn't let me anywhere near her and Julian made it pretty plain that I needed to fuck off and let Mags deal with her."

"Probably for the best," Murf said, "It's what Robbie would do."

Griff rolled his eyes at me and I couldn't help grinning back at him.

But the question that no-one, not even Robbie could answer, was whether or not Ashley would be backstage after the show.

---

*A*shley
      Mags had my total attention. She'd been relaying a story from her early days on tour with Julian.

"So you see," she said "we'd been cooped up in the tour bus and Jules demanded that we stop at a roadside rest stop. We had a journalist on board who'd been documenting his every move for days and we were all getting a little stir-crazy, like you do when you're on the road."

I couldn't imagine being on the road and I struggled with the concept.

"How do you get through?" I asked.

She shrugged. "You just know that it's coming to an end and you try to keep a sense of perspective. You live your life in a fishbowl and remembering that you're public property helps."

Mags stopped to take another sip of her drink and then carried on, a faraway look in her eyes, she obviously enjoyed life on the road with Julian and the band, that was clear even to me in this short amount of time that we'd been conversing.

"So Jules pulls his cock out on the side of the road and starts pissing on a tree."

"No!"

"Oh yes! My reaction exactly. And what's worse the journalist arrived and started taking photos. I tried to stop him and Jules told me to stop."

I couldn't imagine how I'd feel if Paul did something like that.

"No way. What did you do?"

"I got pissed off with Jules and stormed off."

"I can understand that reaction." No wonder they sent Mags in to talk to me.

"He chased after me. Found me crying at the top of the hill. I wasn't even sure why I was crying."

"I think I know why," I said thinking about my own reaction to seeing me and Paul on his channel.

"He explained to me on that hill that afternoon that he was a rockstar who lived on the road," Mags said, "and his public deserved to have a part of his life. The part he gave them wasn't all of him."

I nodded.

"Do you understand what I'm trying to say?" Mags asked.

"The video isn't just Paul, it's me as well," I countered.

"But you have control over how much you give them," Mags said. "That's why we have press conferences and that's why we allow people backstage. It's part of the job."

"His fans want me on stage tonight. I don't think I can do that."

"Do you trust, Paul?" she asked me.

Did I trust, Paul? Wasn't that the question I'd been asking since I'd cut myself off from him this afternoon?

Did I trust Paul to be a good father?

Did I trust Paul to be a good partner?

Never mind trusting Paul. Did I trust myself to be able to cope with this kind of lifestyle?

After careful consideration, I answered the questions. "Yes, I trust him."

Mags smiled at me.

"Well then. I can tell you that he'll look after you on stage. Those boys are a family when they go out there every night. They might have their scraps backstage, or when we're on the road, but when they assemble out there, in front of their fans, they're a unit. Not one of them will let you down if you go out there tonight. I can promise you that."

It was a lot to think about.

Mags stood up. "Only you can decide, Ashley whether you want to be a part of this. It takes a special woman to love a man who gives himself to so many other people night after night. Maybe you need to think about whether or not you're that kind of woman."

She made her way to the door. "Like I said before. If you want to go back to your apartment, you come and find me and I'll arrange for someone to get you home safe. Okay?"

I nodded staring at my hands. "Yes."

"But, Ashley," I looked up into calm and caring eyes. I wondered what Mags had seen on the road. Whether I was able to be the kind of woman that she was. Whether or not I could cope with the rigours of long absences, or even longer periods touring. I'd come to see that it took so much more than just loving a rockstar to stay with him.

"Whatever you decide, you need to let Paul know one way or the other. He deserves that much from you."

With those words hanging in the air, she left me alone with my thoughts.

CHAPTER 19

*P*aul

Now I'd straightened things out with Griff, I needed to find Ashley. I didn't care anymore what Julian or Mags had to say. This was between me and Ashley and we had to get a few things straight.

I found Mags and Julian sitting in the backstage lounge with their daughter and the nanny. The sight of the four of them sitting around stopped me in my tracks.

I took a moment—just to watch the interaction between the four of them. A quaint domestic scene played out in front of me that wouldn't have been out of place in a suburban home.

Their little girl had a sippy cup in her hand. Occasionally she would stop drinking from the cup and shake it around in the air. Tiny droplets of liquid sprayed across her parents. Julian wiped his forehead with the back of his hand and gently admonished his daughter for spraying him. The adoration with which the tiny human being looked up at him would not have been out of place from one of his fans.

Annabelle clearly adored her father.

Mags watched the scene unfolding in front of her with the same intensity that the fans watched Sam and the band on stage. The male nanny, Ed busied himself arranging clothing and food on the table. The same table that Julian and I had our discussion around earlier. Tonight, that horizontal surface would probably be filled with alcohol and god only knew what kind of illegal substances, but right this minute, it hosted a simple family scene.

Julian looked up, caught my eye and the soft edges left his face. "You and the boys sorted?"

"Yeah. Sorted," I replied. "Where's Ashley?"

Before either of them had a chance to answer, a voice said from the other side of the room, "I'm here," and she stepped out of the shadows. She'd been watching Julian and Mags as well.

My stomach clenched at the thought.

Then an overwhelming sense of relief washed over me as Ashley walked towards me.

"Can we talk?" I asked.

"I'd like that," she replied. How long had she been watching the domestic scene in front of us?

"Go use our van," Mags said. "We'll be here for at least another half an hour trying to convince this girl that eating dinner is a good idea."

"Thanks." I held my hand out to Ashley.

She didn't hesitate to take it and I let out a breath that I didn't know I'd been holding.

I squeezed her hand. "Okay?"

Ashley screwed up her face, "Maybe."

I gave her hand another squeeze and walked her out to Julian and Mags' van. I knew that if I'd taken her back to my van Murf and Griff would have vacated and let us have some time alone, but this seemed to be a better option. At least she hadn't run out on me. I had to be grateful for that concession.

"I'm glad you're still here," I said as I opened the door to Mags and Julian's van. It was a replica of the van that me and the boys travelled in, only it didn't have the overwhelming scent of seven-month-old laundry.

Ashley sat down and picked up a small plastic frog that lay on the table in the middle of the van. The whole area was littered with children's toys and assorted bright paraphernalia.

"I guess this is what it looks like traveling on the road with a family," she said.

"They seem to manage well," I agreed thinking about the scene that we'd both witnessed backstage.

"Ed, their nanny seems nice."

"He is," I assured her, "apparently he's been with them forever. An old friend of Mags from years ago."

Ashley continued to roll the brightly coloured frog in her hands, deep in thought. I let the silence sit between us. It wasn't an uncomfortable silence. Nothing about being around Ashley had ever been uncomfortable that was one of the reasons that I'd been so drawn to her.

"Mags talked to me," she said.

"I know."

"Did you send her in?" I noted the defensive tone in Ashley's voice.

I couldn't help but laugh. "No way. Mags and Julian had it worked out between them. Mags took you and Julian took me. They're a devastating tag team."

A delightful smile crept across Ashley's face and I was again reminded of the reason that I'd fallen so totally in love with this woman. It wasn't just the way she looked when she smiled, or the fact that whenever I was around her, I felt so at ease with life. It was also that she understood me. She understood me in a way that I don't think I even understood myself.

"Do you know that until you came along," I said, "nothing mattered to me in the world except my music."

Ashley continued to turn the little green frog around in her hands.

"What matters to you now?" She put the tiny plastic creature down on the table in front of her and focussed on me with a laser-like intensity.

My breath caught in my throat.

I went to open my mouth and no sound would come.

"I'm sorry," Ashley said picking up the frog again, "I didn't mean to put you on the spot." She put the frog down again and picked up a small yellow dress. It had a large blue flower embroidered on the front and I watched in fascination as Ashley traced the ridge of the embroidery with her fingers.

"You and the baby are the most important things in the world to me." I said, the words coming in a rush that I knew I could never take back. Not that I wanted to take them back because they were the truth.

Ashley's head shot up and our eyes caught across the tiny table. The intensity of our gaze seemed to suck the air out of the space we inhabited.

"Your music?"

"My music's important to me, it always will be. But I want everything. I want you and the baby and my music. But if you don't think that you can be a part of my life on the road, then I'll give it up."

I swallowed. I hadn't expected it to be so hard to get the words out of my mouth. Now they were out, there was no taking them back.

Ashley stared at me.

Then she blinked her eyes in rapid fire—trying to comprehend the words that I'd just said. I watched in fascination as she scrunched the dress up in her fists. As if holding onto the material might ground her somehow.

Minutes passed and nothing in the van moved except for the rhythmic opening and closing of Ashley's hands.

Then something inside of her head must have registered. She realised what she was doing with her hands and smoothed the material out on the table in front of her. All the while saying nothing.

I'd just told her that I'd give this all up. Give up my dreams—my life—for her and our baby and she hadn't said a word.

I could feel the heat building inside of my body.

A slow, combustible burn. Reaching out of me. Threatening to overwhelm me.

I needed to connect with Ashley more than I'd ever needed to connect with her before.

Some kind of acknowledgement of the massive concession I'd just made for her.

Anything.

I opened my mouth to speak, but before the words came, Ashley's voice filled the space between us.

"It was while I stood against the wall, backstage, watching Mags and Julian with their little girl that I could see for the first time that there might be a chance for us."

She traced her hands again across the blue flower on the dress as she pressed the creases out that she'd made.

"I wanted to leave tonight after I saw that video." She turned to face me and I saw the pain in her eyes. "I wanted to hate you. I stood in that bathroom and wished for a moment that I'd never set eyes on you in Vegas and that we'd never had that night together."

My insides twisted into a tight knot in response to Ashley's words.

The room began to swim in front of my eyes.

The heat that had been building inside of me erupted out in a hot, soaking sweat.

I stood up, took a faltering step towards her, but she put her hand up, palm facing me. Stopping me.

"Let me finish. Please."

The anguish in the last word was enough to set me back down in my seat.

Sweat trickled down between my shoulder-blades.

All I wanted to do was cross the room and crush Ashley to me.

Instead, I nodded, wordlessly encouraging her to finish what she'd started to say. It hurt me more than anything in the world to sit here and watch the pain and shame play across Ashley's beautiful face.

I wanted to tell her that I wasn't responsible for the video. That all I'd wanted to do was hit Griff. That Julian made me make up with him—but then I realised that a large part of the last thought wasn't exactly the truth. No matter what was going to happen, I would have made it up with Griff. The boys I travelled with on the road were more than band mates, they were like blood brothers. We might have our scrapes and our moments, but we would always look out for each other.

How could I explain what Griff had done he'd done for the band?

Would it make any difference at all now that I'd told Ashley I'd give it all up for her?

Was she going to ask me to give it all up?

A large lump formed in my throat.

I took a deep, ragged breath. "Go on," I said in a voice that barely sounded like my own. For the first time in my life, I put my own need and discomfort aside and encouraged Ashley to tell me her thoughts.

She folded the dress neatly and put it on the table next to the green frog, then turned her attention fully back to me.

"While I stood in the bathroom and after Mags had been in and spoken to me, I realised that there was no way I could walk away from you."

I exhaled.

The air making a whooshing sound as it left my body.

I hadn't even realised I'd been holding my breath.

My body went limp. My clothes stuck to my back. I felt as if I'd just spent two hours on stage.

"Mags helped me to understand the kind of life you live. The way you all compartmentalise your lives. How your fans only see so much of you."

Ashley still hadn't told me whether or not she wanted me to give up touring.

"Then I watched Mags and Julian with their daughter. I can tell by watching Julian how much he loves being on the road. But it was so obvious to me tonight how much he loves Mags and his daughter. I can see that the two things don't have to be mutually exclusive. If Julian can have both worlds, then I guess that means you can have both worlds as well."

What was she saying?

I tipped my head to one side.

Was she saying it was all going to be okay? That we could be on the road together?

Ashley stood up and walked over to me.

Her hands felt cool as they slid across the stubble on my cheeks.

"You see," she said, as she climbed onto my lap, "Julian's not the only one who can have his life on the road and have a family."

Ashley's lips slid over mine and I closed my eyes. Surrendering to the sensual embrace.

When our lips parted, she whispered, "You can too."

I opened my eyes and stared into pools of dark brown.

"Are you sure about this?"

"More sure than I've ever been about anything in my life."

I pulled her to me. Crushing her body against mine.

Joy and relief mingling in the sweet scent of her body.

Nothing would come between me and Ashley and the family that we were creating together—I would make damn sure of it.

"You won't want for anything, I promise," I said as I pulled Ashley's mouth down on my own.

Her lips parted and her body relaxed against mine.

Her touch felt like coming home.

*a*shley
        My body trembled.

I could hear my heart beating hard in my chest.

Slick perspiration coated my skin.

I'd watched Sam and Dusty do their familiar routine on stage and I knew that it was getting closer and closer to Paul's set.

"You okay?" Mags sidled up beside me.

"I don't think so," I said trying to get my uncooperative body under control. She gave me a reassuring hug. "I can't stop shaking."

"You'll be okay when you get out there. All you have to do is go and stand by Paul. He'll hold your hand, introduce you to everyone and then you can walk off."

"I don't have to stay and count the press-ups?"

"If you want to you can. But if you don't, just walk off stage. It's okay, the boys will improvise."

"How many people are out there?"

"About twenty-odd thousand tonight."

"Oh, my god." I could scarcely catch my breath and now I

wanted to vomit. My morning sickness had come under some semblance of control since I'd been holed up in the hotel suite with Paul, but the prospect of standing out there with him in front of twenty plus thousand people. Well, my insides went back into overdrive.

"You won't see them. The house lights are down. You'll hear them, that's all."

"Have you done this?" I asked Mags. For the life of me I still couldn't understand why Paul's fans wanted me out on the stage. Surely, in their eyes, I was just another groupie that would be sidelined as soon as the band rolled out to the next city.

"Lots," she gave me another squeeze. "You'll be a natural in no time."

"You think?"

"I know," she replied, "and besides, the fans will tire of you quick enough so don't get too het up about it."

"Really?" I didn't know whether to be relieved or pissed off.

Mags patted me on the arm, the same way my mom patted me on the arm when I didn't like the piece of advice that she'd just given me.

My mom and dad. I hadn't thought about them since earlier today. I was going to take Paul to meet them tomorrow. As I watched him out on stage a warm sense of connection began to crawl through me. No matter what they thought of him, the fact of the matter was that I loved Paul and we were going to make a family together.

The thought filled me with a sense of overwhelming pleasure that I had never expected to feel. Maybe if I kept my focus on the warm feelings, I wouldn't feel so nervous and self-conscious. Paul had done nothing except put me at ease from the moment that I'd met him.

A sudden memory of that meeting in the heat of Vegas washed over me.

Maybe it was a flush of fear.

A stage manager arrived at our side.

Headphones and a small microphone adorned his head.

"Ready?" he asked as he lightly touched my forearm.

Mags gave me a nod and waited for my response.

"As I'll ever be," I replied.

"All set back stage," he said into the microphone.

No sooner had he said the words than Paul stepped forward toward the cheering crowd.

I watched in what seemed like slow motion as he began to work his way through the routine that I'd witnessed a couple of times now. Then he turned and walked towards me.

I felt a hand in the small of my back. I didn't know whether it was Mags or the stage manager. It didn't matter.

I could barely breathe.

As I stepped out from between the screens that ran along the side of the stage I felt as if I was walking through treacle.

Paul flicked the hair from across his eye, so that he looked at me squarely with both of them. A smile erupted on his face and in that moment, as his hand reached out and he took mine, I knew I loved him more than anyone I'd ever loved in my life.

Even if we had to play this charade of a relationship out in the public eye, I knew I was prepared to do that.

Not just for the baby—but because I wanted this.

I wanted to be a part of this crazy, unpredictable life on the road.

"You up for this?" Paul asked as he squeezed my hand.

"Yes," I replied.

"Come and meet the fans," he said as he walked me to the centre of the stage.

All I could hear was the deafening roar of my own name.

"Ashley! Ashley! Ashley!" They chanted.

For the first time, I had an inkling of why these boys stood up here every night.

The hair on the back of my neck stood on end.

Adrenaline spiked through my body.

My heart began to race and I felt a broad smile appear of its own accord. Now I knew what it felt like to have the entire crowd behind you. What a thrill it must be for Paul to have this kind of adoration thrown at him night after night.

It dawned on me in that millisecond what it was that he'd said he would give up.

For me.

For our child.

I looked at him in a new and beautiful light.

He squeezed my hand again and then let it go.

"What say you?" I heard Sam say to the audience.

"Count! Count! Count!" Came the chant from the crowd.

Paul pulled his shirt over his head and threw it at me.

I caught it and the crowd roared their approval.

Sam winked at me and I felt the fear evaporate.

I'd spent time with these guys. They were having fun on stage. My body began to relax.

Without thinking about it, I put my foot on Paul's back and pushed him down into his first press-up.

"You go, girl!" Dusty called from the other side of the stage.

And so it went.

Now the initial fear had receded, the minutes I spent on stage flew by in what seemed like seconds.

When Paul pulled me into a bear hug and almost squeeze the air out of my lungs, the crowd erupted—the sound washing across the stage in undulating waves. I gave him back his shirt and as he shimmied it back on, Sam pulled me towards him and made me take a bow.

A flush of heat rushed through my body, as Paul put his arm around me, turned me for one last wave at the crowd and escorted me to the side of the stage.

I couldn't be sure whether the heat that ran through me was due to the thrill of being on stage, or because of the fact that Paul had shown more than twenty thousand people his love for me.

In any case it didn't matter.

"You were great," Mags exclaimed as I stood breathless at the edge of the stage. Paul threw me another wink as he pulled his bass back across his body and readied himself for the next song.

"It all happened so fast," I replied and I wasn't sure whether I was talking about the time I'd spent on stage or my split-second decision that no matter what happened going forward, I wanted to be a part of Paul's life on the stage and on the road.

---

*E*pilogue - Paul

Post-show we were installed back at the hotel. The band had been buzzing and Ashley had caught the buzz —real bad.

I'd showered already and Ashley lay in the huge double bed in the middle of the suite. When I walked in the room, she put the tablet down on the bedside cabinet and turned her attention to me.

"They love us," she said.

"You shouldn't be looking at that social media shit," I teased, "it rots your brain."

"It's entirely responsible for your fame and fortune," she teased me back.

"Some of it has to do with how well I play bass." I tried to sound indignant, but Ashley's laughter filled the room.

I couldn't believe how well things had gone when she was on stage. The crowd loved her and she loved being there. *That must bode well for the future*, a tiny voice in my head whispered. I told it to shut up. I'd told Ashley I would happily give up touring if that was what she wanted me to do. She might be filled with the flush of post-show adrenaline now, but being on the road could be exhausting. Touring was what I'd worked my arse off to achieve—touring was what I'd wanted more than anything else in life—until I met Ashley.

If future touring meant having to give up Ashley, then I was prepared to quit for her and the baby. I didn't know how I'd manage being a regular guy with a regular job but I'd do it to keep Ashley in my life.

I climbed into the bed alongside her and basked in the pleasant sensation of nakedness beside me. Her body did things to me that I'd never experienced with anyone else.

"You were fantastic out there tonight," I said to Ashley as I ran my fingers through her long, blonde hair.

"You think?" she asked.

"I know," I said. "Everybody loved you. The band thought you were fantastic. You could be a permanent fixture if this was what you wanted."

"I don't think so," she replied. "I think it's just being here in Seattle. They love their own in this town. Besides, Mags told me that the fans would get bored with me as soon as the novelty wore off."

"Don't underestimate your own ability to perform. That moment you put your foot on my back was a piece of pure brilliance."

Ashley snorted back a laugh. "I'm just practising for having you permanently under my thumb," she said as her hand cupped my balls.

A sweet sensation of lust rushed through my body.

I loved the sound of the word permanent. How permanent was our life going to be together? And where was that permanent life going to be located? I was waiting for Ashley to tell me.

She leaned into me, the softness of her large breast brushing against the side of my body. The subtle movement of the curves of her body sent another bolt of lust curling through my insides. It was a feeling that I'd never tire of.

Ashley's fingers began to trace the rose tattoo across my heart. I knew the hues and colour on my body fascinated her. I loved the feel of her fingers and the way she traced them along the lines of ink.

The sensation began to lull me into a sensual stupor.

"What would you say if I said that I'd be happy to come on the road with you permanently?" Her fingers stopped moving as she waited for my answer.

I opened my eyes and stared into intense pools of brown. "I'd say that you've made me the happiest man alive tonight." I took a breath. Ashley seemed to be holding hers. "You sure about what you're saying?" I stroked the smooth skin of Ashley's back and she nodded her affirmation. "It's a pretty hard life being on the road. I mean, we'd have our own van and everything, but we wouldn't be holed up in hotels like this the whole time."

"I think I could manage," she replied as she pressed her lips to the rose on my chest. "I've been watching Mags and Julian and they seem to be doing okay, so I don't see any reason why we shouldn't be okay as well."

"But what about your parents?" I thought about our meeting tomorrow. Telling them Ashley was pregnant was going to be bad enough. Now I was encouraging their daughter to run away with the circus that was a rock band on the road. "Have you thought about what they might have to say?"

She pressed herself up on her elbow, her eyes level with mine. "You're going to meet them, but I really don't care what they have to say. I know where I want to be. I know that I want our child to have two parents and for that to happen, I'm going on the road with you."

"I meant it when I said I'd give up touring."

"But music and touring are part of you," Ashley said, her eyes wide. "I saw that tonight. If I asked you to give that up then I'd be asking you to give up the part of you that fascinates me. The essence of you. I'd be left with no more than a dried up bitter shell of a man."

Ashley stroked my hair across my forehead. "I could never do that to you. So that means I'm gonna be with you on the road whether you like it or not."

My heart ached.

My throat ached.

My head felt as if it was going to explode.

"I love you," I whispered, the words lost in Ashley's mouth as I slanted my lips over hers and immersed myself in the woman who made my life complete.

ABOUT THE AUTHOR

Hello from Auckland, New Zealand.

Thank you so much for taking the time out of your busy life to read my story. I do hope that you enjoyed following Paul and Ashley as they worked their way through their turbulent romance.

How do you think Paul will manage when Ashley gives birth to their baby? If you'd like to know, then make sure you sign up at http://eepurl.com/cYb0jH to receive the bonus story. What do you think Paul's chances are of keeping the fans on his channel in the birth loop? We all know Ashley's pretty adamant that she's not going to be in the spotlight—but what about their baby? Once you've signed up, keep an eye on your inbox for your bonus story.

I love writing about rockstars. Many of you will know that I come from a musical family and that my husband is *cough* a bass player—no he's nothing like Paul!

I am also the daughter of a bass player, so you could say that I have a soft spot for men who play guitars with four (or sometimes five) strings.

I am very much looking forward to completing the Style

Strike series and will be visiting with our reprobate drummer—Todd (Murf) Murphy—very soon.

I love meeting my readers (old and new) so do make sure that you drop me an email and say hello. I always reply to my readers.

For anyone who doesn't know where New Zealand is, we're sitting below Australia at the bottom of the world. It's a fantastic place to live and I'm so blessed to call this peaceful piece of paradise home.

Hope to catch up with you soon.

Until then, take care.

Love Toni x

PS If you'd like your very own backstage pass, don't forget to come and visit with us on Facebook at the private Red Couch group. You'll find us all hanging out here: https://www.facebook.com/groups/romanceredcouch

For more information about Toni Kenyon:

www.tonikenyon.com
toni@tonikenyon.com

ALSO BY TONI KENYON

PRIVATE LOVE IN A PUBLIC PLACE

Mags O'Brien lives on the alcohol-soaked, drug-enhanced concert circuit, managing out-of-control rocker Julian MacAvoy. She helps him spread his musical gospel to his adoring followers, despite the fast-spinning turnstile on his bedroom door, and the broken hearts he leaves in his wake.

Mags believes she's immune to Julian's magnetic personality but when controversy hits the tour, she finds herself in danger of falling at his feet, slave to his appetites and her own desire and need.

Julian refuses to be tamed, but the pressure of the ravenous crowds clamps tighter and tighter around him. His chaotic world starts to crumble when he realises his motivation to continue touring comes from an unobtainable woman. Can he force her to make the agonising choice between himself and her estranged husband?

An erotic and candid look at life on the road.

Download your copy Private Love in a Public Place

Praise for PRIVATE LOVE IN A PUBLIC PLACE

I'm a huge fan of Rock&Roll love stories. This one rates right up there with Olivia Cunning's "Sinners" & "Sole Regret" and "FitzWilliam Darcy". I can't wait for the 2nd book to come out in April! This story has it all... Heartbreak, Steamy but Very Real love and really tough choices. At one point, I cried like a baby and in the next, I was yelling at my KindleFire. LoL...

Bottom line- Totally worth adding this book to your collection!

Sexy and gritty, raw and engaging, "Private Love in a Public Place" takes you on a personal behind-the-scenes tour of a rock star's life on the road from the perspective of his manager, a woman who loves the artist as much as she loves the man himself. ... This is a fresh, steamy and surprising love story guaranteed to entertain!

Mags is open and real, a woman I could relate too in a job many of us would see as glamorous (manager to a rock star or babysitter perhaps) but which she made very real, faults and all. Jules is that mix of arrogant tosser and little boy lost, who you can't help but fall in love with. A rock star who shows us he's human.

Other work from Toni Kenyon

CATCH

Tamsen Parsons is happy with her wacky world. So she leases fish to big business, her bedroom resembles a gypsy fortune-teller's caravan and she's got the flat-mate from hell. Still, the sun's shining and she can smile.

That is until uptight lawyer Matthew Solomon breaks into her serene world. He's over the corporate climb, unsure what he wants in life anymore and the sexy and aloof Tamsen looks like just the sort of short-term tonic he needs.

What Matt doesn't count on is his interfering mother, Tamsen's out-of-control best friend and falling in love.

Can a gypsy-fish-minder really bring this bad-boy to heel?

Download your copy Catch

Praise for CATCH:

Wonderfully written and will read over and over again. Definitely one to tell others to read as well. A Keeper.

Kenyon writes a sexy, fast paced, contemporary romance that'll have your heart racing. Tamsen is a terrific heroine with a unique job (nice change from the usual romance heroine) and Matt is definitely a hot hero worthy of her. The sensuality is scorching hot, so be warned you'll need a long cold drink in hand when reading Catch. Kudos to Toni Kenyon for a marvelous story - definitely an author to watch!

This book keeps you wanting to read more. Once you think you have it figured out, you get thrown for a loop.

RETURN TO ALA MOANA BEACH

Ty Carter's an expert bomb disposal technician who doesn't take anything lying down. But a bullet to the back cuts short his tour in Iraq, returning him to a wife who he believes deserves more than half-a-man as a husband.

Lulu Carter wants nothing more than the man she married to come home. Instead, an injured and disturbed stranger turns life upside down for her and their children.

Only Ty and Lulu can decide if the love they shared is worth fighting for and whether they should stay married after such a traumatic event.

Download your copy Return to Ala Moana Beach

Praise for RETURN TO ALA MOANA BEACH:

Amazing book, couldn't put it down. their separation was heartbreaking...but it's a lovely story and shows the reality that many soldiers went through...

A beautiful and moving story about what happens after a soldier comes home. The characters and the gorgeous setting illustrate a realistic and lovely world. Hawaii is a character by itself. Not only does the author portray the returning soldier well, but she does an excellent job describing the feelings and thoughts of his family. The story revolves around the veteran's trauma, but also everyone who cares about him. I love it.

www.ingramcontent.com/pod-product-compliance
Lightning Source LLC
Chambersburg PA
CBHW060931180626
46817CB00004B/I489